PETER C
CALLING MR. CALLAGHAN

REGINALD Evelyn Peter Southouse Cheyney (1896-1951) was
born in Whitechapel in the East End of London. After serving
as a lieutenant during the First World War, he worked as
a police reporter and freelance investigator until he found
success with his first Lemmy Caution novel. In his lifetime
Cheyney was a prolific and wildly successful author, selling, in
1946 alone, over 1.5 million copies of his books. His work was
also enormously popular in France, and inspired Jean-Luc
Godard's character of the same name in his dystopian sci-fi
film *Alphaville*. The master of British noir, in Lemmy Caution
Peter Cheyney created the blueprint for the tough-talking,
hard-drinking pulp fiction detective.

PETER CHEYNEY

CALLING MR. CALLAGHAN

DEAN STREET PRESS

Published by Dean Street Press 2022

All Rights Reserved

First published in 1953

Cover by DSP

ISBN 978 1 915014 19 1

www.deanstreetpress.co.uk

1
A SPOT OF MURDER

WHEN Callaghan came into the office, Effie Thompson stopped typing. She said: "Good morning, Mr. Callaghan. There have been a few telephone calls, and your letters are on your desk."

Callaghan said: "Right, Effie. Has Fallon or Craske been through?"

She shook her head. Callaghan went into his office. She followed him with her notebook.

She said: "You're expecting a call from Fallon or Craske? If either of them come through while you're out what shall I do about it?"

Callaghan said: "There's nothing you can do, Effie. Both those birds ought to be pretty scared by this time—both of them or one of them."

She said: "You don't know which one was really responsible for that fraudulent claim?"

Callaghan said: "No! But with the situation like it is, I bet the guilty one's feeling scared and the innocent one is beginning to get ideas." He lit a cigarette. "Of course," he went on, "there's a chance they were both concerned in it."

He began to dictate his letters.

The telephone jangled. Effie Thompson took off the receiver. She put her hand over the transmitter. She said: "Talk of the devil! Mr. Fallon wants to speak to you, Mr. Callaghan."

Callaghan reached out for the instrument. He said: "Hello, Fallon. What is it?"

Fallon said: "Look, Mr. Callaghan, I've been thinking things over and I think I've got them straightened out. I think I'm in a position to prove that Craske—my partner—has been the person who double-crossed the Insurance Company. I can prove I had nothing to do with it."

Callaghan said: "I'm glad of that, Fallon. You know we never accused you of anything."

Fallon said: "I know. At the same time I realized you probably suspected the pair of us. After all, no Insurance Company likes to pay twenty thousand on a fake claim, and I'm afraid that's what it was."

Callaghan said: "That's what I thought." There was a pause. Then: "What do you want me to do?" he asked.

Fallon said: "Look here, circumstances have broken pretty well for me. Craske went off this morning and took the train for Newcastle. So he'll be out of the way. All the books and everything are in the safe down here on the houseboat. I went through them directly he left a couple of hours ago, and with the information that I've got I can show you just how he did it."

Callaghan said: "You want me to come down?"

Fallon said: "Yes. I'd like to do a few more hours' work on the books, but if you could get down this evening about nine o'clock, I think I'd have the whole thing straightened out."

Callaghan said: "All right. I'll be there. I'm glad you've got yourself in the clear, Fallon. I knew it had to be *one* of you, but, of course, there was always the chance that it was *both* of you. I'll be with you at nine o'clock."

"Right ho!" said Fallon. "The houseboat is moored by the landing stage oil the road about a hundred and fifty yards from the Star & Crown. Anybody'll tell you where it is. I'll be there."

Callaghan asked: "Where are you speaking from?"

"From the Star & Crown," Fallon answered.

Callaghan said: "All right." He hung up. He stubbed out his cigarette, lit a fresh one. He said to Effie Thompson: "Fallon says he's got the goods on his partner Craske. He says he can prove it was Craske who pulled that fake claim. Fallon wants to see me. I'm going down to the houseboat to see him at nine o'clock to-night."

Effie Thompson said: "Are you going on your own? It might be a plant, mightn't it? You've only got Fallon's word that it was Craske who was responsible for the fraud."

Callaghan said: "That's true enough. At the same time you've got to take a chance sometime. But thanks for being concerned, Effie." He blew ruminative smoke rings. Then he went on: "I suppose there might be something in this thing called woman's intuition."

She smiled. She said: "Every woman thinks so, Mr. Callaghan."

"All right," said Callaghan. "Take this note down. I'm going out in a few minutes, so I shan't be here when Nikolls arrives. When he comes in give him the note."

She said: "Very well, Mr. Callaghan."

Callaghan dictated the note.

A sharp wind was blowing and a few big rain spots fell as Callaghan, leaving the road by the Inn, turned off on to the footpath that ran down to the river's edge. After a few minutes' walking he could see in the dusk the outline of the houseboat moored to the bank in the little backwater.

He paused a moment to light a cigarette, then continued on his way. He reached the houseboat, stepped aboard. There was no sign of life. Callaghan called out: "Fallon!" There was no reply.

He walked along the side of the boat until he came to the main door. It was unlocked. Callaghan pushed it open. It was quite dark inside, the windows being screened by black-out curtains. Callaghan put his hand on to the wall by the door, felt for an electric light switch. He found it, snapped it on. At the other end of the cabin, behind a desk, sat Craske. The automatic in his right hand was pointed at Callaghan's stomach.

He said: "Come in, Callaghan. Close the door behind you. I want to have a little talk with you."

Callaghan grinned. He said: "So it seems. This is a surprise, Craske."

Craske said: "I bet it is. Sit down, Callaghan, in that chair and keep your hands on the arms. Don't take any chances."

Callaghan said sarcastically: "I don't intend to take any chances."

Craske said: "You thought you were going to see Fallon, didn't you?"

Callaghan nodded. He said: "Do you mind if I give myself another cigarette?"

Craske said: "No, I don't mind anything so long as you don't try anything funny."

Callaghan stubbed out his cigarette end. He produced his cigarette case, lit a fresh cigarette. He inhaled from the cigarette, then he said: "Yes, I thought I was going to see Fallon, and I thought you were in Newcastle. It seems I was wrong."

Craske said: "Yes. But Fallon wasn't kidding you."

Callaghan raised one eyebrow. "No?" he queried. There was a pause. Then: "What's the idea in the gun, Craske?" he asked. "That sort of stuff isn't going to get you anywhere."

"Oh yes, it is," said Craske. "I'm sorry, Callaghan, but I'm going to kill you. You see, I've got to."

Callaghan said: "You don't say! Why?"

Craske said: "I'll tell you. I got the idea some time ago that Fallon was wise to what I'd been doing. I got the idea that he'd been checking up on what had been going on." He grinned. "I knew he'd been going through the firm's books which I had down here over the weekend," he went on. "He thought I didn't know. Fallon's a bit of a mug, you know."

Callaghan said: "You're telling me. But any man would have to be pretty clever to be your partner, Craske."

"Maybe," said Craske. "Anyhow, I came to the conclusion he was going to do something about it. So I thought I'd give him the opportunity. I told him this morning I was going up to Newcastle. Then I packed my bag and cleared off. I went along to the Star & Crown. I went upstairs to the first floor landing and watched to see if Fallon would come along and telephone after he'd had a chance of going through those books."

"He did. He telephoned from the box downstairs." He grinned. "There's never anybody in the office on the first floor in the morning. I knew that that manageress is always downstairs in the kitchen at that time. I went into the office. I listened on the extension line. I heard him fixing up for you to come down to-night. I heard what he said."

Callaghan nodded. "Nice work," he said.

"Not too bad," said Craske. "When he'd gone I went downstairs, rang for a car, drove to the station, picked up the Newcastle train. I was careful to let the porter see that I actually caught it. You see I happened to know the train stops for water on this side of the Blackwood Tunnel—twelve miles away."

Callaghan nodded. "And when the train stopped you just got out?"

"That's right," said Craske. "I waited till seven o'clock this evening, then I telephoned Fallon at the Star & Crown—I knew he'd be there for dinner—and told him his mother was dying. I made out I was a friend of his mother's. I knew that would move him, and I knew he wouldn't telephone your office because he'd know it'd be closed. Half an hour ago I slipped back here and waited for you. No one saw me."

Callaghan drew easily on his cigarette. He said: "All very interesting. And what's the big idea?"

"The big idea is this," said Craske. "You'll be dead. I was seen on the train going to Newcastle to-day, so I'm all right. Your office know that you had an appointment here with Fallon at nine o'clock. Fallon will say that he wasn't here—he went to see his mother who was dying. Who's going to believe him. His mother's not dying, and she's not even at the address I gave him." He smiled. "I gave him the address of an empty house. You get the idea?"

Callaghan said: "I get it. The idea is that the Insurance Company I'm working for know that I suspected both of you as being in this job. They'll believe Fallon killed me. You'll have an alibi and Fallon's alibi won't stand up—it's obviously a fake."

Craske nodded. He said: "That's right."

Callaghan said: "Nice work! I congratulate you, Craske. Just because Fallon's alibi is so obviously a fake—although it was the truth—the police won't check too carefully on your alibi which looks good although it's a fake. All they'll do is to check you got on that Newcastle train." He nodded appreciatively. "You know, Craske," he went on, "it's not at all a bad idea. In point of fact it's almost watertight. It's really very hard luck on you that you won't get away with it."

Craske said almost casually: "What's the good of bluffing, Callaghan? You'd better make up your mind to take what's coming to you." He leveled the gun. "I'm going to give it to you in a minute," he said. "Perhaps you'd like to turn round?"

Callaghan said: "I wouldn't even bother. But you'd be awfully silly if you squeezed that trigger before I told you what I'm going to tell you. After all, it's not so bad doing five or six years imprisonment for making a fraudulent insurance claim, but it would be just too bad to be hanged for an unnecessary murder."

Craske said: "What do you mean—an unnecessary murder?" He looked surprised.

Callaghan said: "I'll tell you. I said your idea was very nearly watertight. But you see the unfortunate thing was that Fallon never got anywhere near that empty house where you told him his dying mother was. He was knocked over by a car. The hospital phoned through to my office—my secretary happened to be working late. It's too bad," said Callaghan, "because you realize that it will be quite obvious that Fallon didn't kill me the only other person who would have a motive for being on this houseboat and finishing me off would be you. That being so, that Newcastle alibi of yours will be closely checked, which it would not be in the ordinary course of events. They'll discover that you never arrived at Newcastle. You won't be able to tell them who you saw there—what you did there.

"I'm sorry about Fallon," Callaghan went on. "The reason I was a bit late getting here was because I went to the hospital. He died at eight o'clock to-night."

Craske sighed heavily. He put the automatic pistol on the desk. He said: "Well, that lets you out."

Callaghan said: "So you've changed your mind, Craske?"

Craske nodded. He grinned. "Why not?" he said. "Now that Fallon's dead, the situation becomes a little easier. Before he had that telephone conversation with you this morning you've admitted that you suspected both or either of us. Now my story's going to be that it was Fallon who pulled that claim on the Insurance Company. You can say what you like about this interview. Who's going to believe you? My story's as good as yours. They'll never be able to convict me of that fraud in a thousand years, and you know it."

He pulled the ammunition clip out of the butt of the gun, threw the clip and the pistol into the desk drawer. He said: "There's another idea, too." He grinned at Callaghan cynically. "Look," he went on, "my story is going to be that Fallon committed suicide. Here he was this evening in a district that he had no reason to be in, getting knocked down by a motor-car. Maybe he threw himself under that car because he knew he was going to be found out. That's a good story too," Craske concluded.

Callaghan nodded. He said: "It's not bad. You're a clever fellow, Craske."

Craske said: "I think so, too!"

"Well," said Callaghan, "it looks as if I can't do any good staying here. I'll be on my way."

Craske said: "Good-night, Callaghan. I'm not going to do a thing. If the Insurance Company put the police on to me, I've got my story all ready for them, and nobody can prove anything different."

Callaghan got up. He stubbed out his cigarette end in the ashtray on the desk. He walked slowly to the door of the cabin. He opened the door, turned. He stood looking at Craske.

He said: "You know, Craske, life is damn funny. When Fallon rang through to my office this morning I didn't actually believe him. I thought it was a plant. I thought he wanted to get me down here to-night to try something on. So I tried a little idea of my own. Would you like to hear what it was?"

Craske said nothing. He looked at Callaghan.

Callaghan went on: "I left a note for Windemere Nikolls, my assistant, to get down here this afternoon, and if the coast was clear to get a Dictaphone fixed in the wall of this cabin. You might like to know that every word that's been said in here will be produced as evidence. Nikolls got a line running up the bank. He's been sitting there behind a tree with the earphones on ever since I came here."

Craske gasped. He looked at Callaghan as if he had been pole-axed.

"So much for that," said Callaghan. "The other thing is we've got all the evidence we want against you—including Fallon. I shall put Fallon in the witness box against Craske."

Craske said: "What the devil do you mean? Fallon's dead."

Callaghan grinned. He said: "Nuts, Craske! That little story I told you about Fallon being knocked over and killed was phoney. I made that up. Good-night, Craske."

2
DOUBLE ALIBI

NIKOLLS, Callaghan's Canadian assistant, was sitting in the corner of the deserted saloon bar when Callaghan came in. Callaghan went to the bar, ordered a large whisky and soda, carried it over to where Nikolls was sitting. He said: "Well, what was it Vinter wanted? I suppose he thinks he's in a jam?"

Nikolls said: "He's in a jam all right. I told him so. I asked him how the hell he thought a firm of private detectives was goin' to get him out of this one."

Callaghan asked: "What's the story?"

Nikolls finished his whisky and soda. He said: "This guy Charlesworth was shot on the road between his house and Vinter's cottage two nights ago and the police have been snoopin' around plenty. Vinter thinks they're going to arrest him. I think so too. Just how he thinks you're gonna help I don't know."

Callaghan said: "You think he killed Charlesworth?"

Nikolls carried the two empty glasses to the bar, ordered fresh drinks, brought them back. He said: "Listen. This guy Vinter owes Charlesworth a lotta money. Two nights ago Charlesworth heard that Vinter was skippin' to Canada. He went along to see Vinter but he never got there. He was found in the roadway shot, about twenty yards from an A.A. box. It looks like somebody was waitin' for him behind the A.A. box."

Callaghan said: "I see. You think that was Vinter. But what you think isn't evidence."

"That's right enough," said Nikolls. "But this is evidence. Vinter's got a wife, see? He left her six months ago and she don't like him a bit. She's livin' on the other side of Valeham Woods, about five miles away. O.K. Well, on the afternoon of the day that Charlesworth was killed she rang up Mrs. Charlesworth. She said she wanted to speak to her husband. Mrs. Charlesworth said her husband wasn't in. He'd be back about six forty-five. So Mrs. Vinter asked that when he did come in he should ring her, because it was very important. She left her telephone number. You got that?"

Callaghan said: "I've got it."

Nikolls continued: "At about six forty-five Charlesworth gets home. He rings up Mrs. Vinter. Mrs. Vinter tells him she's got an idea that her husband is gonna skip to Canada, that he's gonna take a run-out powder on her and everyone else, and take Charlesworth's dough with him. She says if Charlesworth is gonna do anything about it he'd better get busy. And then she says something else. She tells him to be careful if he's gonna see Vinter. She says Vinter's dangerous. She says that before she left him Vinter told her that ii Charlesworth got funny about his money he'd think nothing of puttin' a bullet into him. Well, is that evidence or is it?"

Callaghan asked: "Do the police know this?"

"You bet they know it," said Nikolls. "Because Charlesworth told his wife what Mrs. Vinter had said on the telephone, before he went out to see Vinter."

Callaghan said: "Well, it doesn't look so good for our client, does it?"

Nikolls nodded. "It certainly does not," he said.

Callaghan asked: "Where was Vinter supposed to be at the time that Charlesworth was killed?"

Nikolls grinned. "He says he was walkin' round the golf course."

Callaghan said: "That's not very good, is it?"

Nikolls said: "You're tellin' me!" He brought out of his pocket an envelope. "There's five hundred pounds in notes in that envelope. That's from Vinter. He says he's heard about you. He thinks you're clever. He says maybe you'll find a way of gettin' him out of this."

Callaghan put the envelope in his pocket. He said: "I don't work for murderers, but you never know. Maybe he didn't do it."

Nikolls said: "Maybe he didn't, but I think he did. He'd got a motive. He'd plenty of reason for wantin' Charlesworth outa the way."

Callaghan asked: "How did Vinter know that Charlesworth was comin' to see him?"

"That's easy," said Nikolls. "The road between Charlesworth's place and Vinter's cottage is a long deserted road. It leads only to the golf course or Vinter's place. Vinter could see down the road from his cottage. If he saw Charlesworth comin' along that road he'd know what he was comin' for, wouldn't he?"

Callaghan said: "It looks to me as if you're right." He finished his drink, got up.

Nikolls said: "What are you gonna do?"

Callaghan said: "I don't know. Just as a start off I think I'll go and see Mrs. Vinter. Where did you say she lives?"

"About five miles away," said Nikolls. "Here's the address."

Callaghan said: "You walk round to the golf club and see if you can pick anything up. Meet me here at seven o'clock to-night."

Mrs. Vinter was a woman who had once been beautiful. Now she looked a little pathetic.

Callaghan said: "I'm sorry to bother you, Mrs. Vinter. I'm a private detective. Your husband has asked me to look after his interests. I expect you know what the position is?"

She nodded. She said: "I suppose he thinks he's going to be arrested?"

Callaghan said: "That's right. He thinks so. So do I. But there's no reason why I shouldn't try to do my job, is there?"

She said: "Well, I hope you think you've a chance of being successful."

Callaghan smiled. He said: "Mrs. Vinter, you don't like your husband, do you?"

She said: "Why should I? I've every reason not to like him, but that doesn't mean that I want to see him tried for murder—unless, of course, he committed that murder."

Callaghan said: "Would you mind telling me exactly what happened on the day that Charlesworth was killed so far as you're concerned?"

She said: "Certainly, Mr. Callaghan. As you probably know, my husband owed Charlesworth a great deal of money. He owed me money too. The evening before, I rang him up on the telephone and asked him what he was going to do about my allowance. He was very rude. He told me he was going to Canada, that he'd be well rid of me, that as far as he was concerned I'd never get another penny from—him. I thought it over and the next day I rang Mrs. Charlesworth. I rang her up in the early evening. I asked to speak to her husband. Apparently he doesn't get back till about six forty-five. I left my telephone number and asked her to get him to call me when he came in. At about six forty-five he rang me up. I told him what I knew. I said that if he wanted to get his money from my husband he'd better get a move on, because I'd heard that my husband was leaving for Canada shortly."

Callaghan said: "I see. What did Charlesworth say?"

"He said he'd go along and have a show-down with my husband," said Mrs. Vinter.

Callaghan nodded. "And then you warned him to be careful. Had you any reason to do that, Mrs. Vinter?"

She said: "Yes, I had every reason. I know my husband. He told me once before that if Charlesworth came and bothered him he'd kill him."

Callaghan said: "But Charlesworth didn't seem to take very much notice of your warning?"

She said: "No. He said he thought that was all bluff on my husband's part."

Callaghan got up. He said: "Well, thank you very much, Mrs. Vinter. I must say it doesn't look very good for your husband. It seems as if things have caught up with him, doesn't it? As far as I can see there's no one else had any motive or opportunity for killing Charlesworth."

She looked out of the window. She said: "I suppose not." There was a note of hesitation in her voice.

Callaghan said: "What's on your mind, Mrs. Vinter? If you know anything else you ought to talk, you know—even if you don't like your husband."

She said: "Perhaps I haven't any right to give voice to my suspicions but when you said there was no one else who had any motive or opportunity—"

Callaghan said: "I see. So there was someone else who had motive and opportunity?"

She smiled. "The only other person who could have known that Charlesworth was going to see my husband would be Mrs. Charlesworth, wouldn't it?"

"Why should Mrs. Charlesworth want to kill her husband?" asked Callaghan.

She smiled. She said: "The usual reason, I should think. Perhaps now, Mr. Callaghan, you know why I haven't lived with my husband for the last six months. Perhaps I told Mr. Charlesworth something else on the telephone. Perhaps there was an additional reason why he should have a show-down with my husband."

Callaghan said: "I see. Are you trying to tell me, Mrs. Vinter, that possibly your husband wasn't going to Canada alone? Are you trying to tell me there was something on between him and Mrs. Charlesworth?"

She said: "I'm not trying to tell you anything, Mr. Callaghan. I've told you all I know. Is there anything else I can do?"

"No, thank you very much," said Callaghan. "I think that's all, except may I use your telephone? I'd like to ring my office. Then I don't think I need worry you any more."

*

It was seven o'clock when Callaghan went into the saloon at the Peacock Inn. Chief Detective-Inspector Gringall, standing at the bar, regarded him with a raised eyebrow.

Callaghan said: "Fancy seeing you down here, Gringall."

Gringall said: "Are you surprised? I've got a murder on my hands. Incidentally, a little bird tells me that Richard Vinter has asked Callaghan Investigations to look after his interests." He smiled a little grimly. "My own opinion is, they'll need some looking after."

Callaghan said: "You might be right." He smiled amiably at Gringall. "I've got an idea that our client is your number one suspect."

Gringall said: "You never know. I suppose you wouldn't have any ideas on the subject?"

Callaghan said: "I'm all for supporting law and order, but there's just one little point that you may have overlooked. Of course, you know all there is to be known. I expect you've seen Mrs. Vinter."

Gringall nodded.

Callaghan went on: "Vinter had motive and opportunity for killing Charlesworth. Don't think I'm trying to draw any red herrings across the path, Gringall, but I've got an idea that although Mrs. Vinter wouldn't mind seeing her husband hanged for killing Charlesworth, she doesn't think in her heart that he did it."

Gringall said: "What do you mean?"

Callaghan said: "I thought that would interest you. I've been talking to Mrs. Vinter. She's got an idea that there was something on between Mrs. Charlesworth and her husband. That rather mixes things up a bit, doesn't it?"

Gringall said: "Well, it might."

Callaghan said: "You see, when Charlesworth called Mrs. Vinter on the telephone she told him something more than the fact that Vinter was skipping to Canada with Charlesworth's money. I believe she suggested that Mrs. Charlesworth might be going too."

Gringall produced a short briar pipe and began to fill it. "I see," he said. "The idea being that having had this telephone conversation, Charlesworth told his wife all about it, told her that he was going to have a show-down with Vinter, that he was going to upset their little plot to get out of the country on his money, and that maybe she didn't like it."

Callaghan said: "That could have happened, couldn't it? You remember Charlesworth was shot a few yards from the A.A. box at the fork. He was shot in the back. Of course, he could have been shot by Vinter, who was waiting for him, from behind the A.A. box. On the other hand, he could have been shot by Mrs. Charlesworth, who could have followed him. Maybe she wasn't too keen on his having that show-down with Vinter."

Gringall said: "You never know."

Callaghan said: "I suppose it would be rude to ask what you propose doing?"

Gringall said: "I'm going to have a little talk with Mrs. Charlesworth. I suppose you'd appreciate it if I asked you to come along."

Callaghan said: "I'd consider it an honour." He grinned at Gringall.

They went out of the bar. They began to walk down the country road in the direction of the Charlesworth house.

Gringall drew on his pipe. He said: "Slim, I know you're working for Vinter. He's probably given you a nice fat fee to try and get him out of this. You wouldn't get up to any funny business, would you?"

Callaghan said: "What . . . me! I couldn't think of such a thing."

Gringall looked at him sideways. "Like hell you couldn't!" he said.

Mrs. Charlesworth was a plump and pleasant woman of forty. Her hair was freshly waved, her frock fashionable. Callaghan looked at her admiringly.

Gringall said: "I'm sorry to bother you, Mrs. Charlesworth. I am Chief Detective-Inspector Gringall, the police officer in charge of this unfortunate business. I'd like to ask you some questions."

She said: "Won't you sit down, gentlemen? Ask anything you want."

Gringall said: "Mrs. Charlesworth, I want you to tell me exactly what happened on the day your husband was killed."

She said: "I'll tell you, Mr. Gringall. In the evening Mrs. Vinter rang up. She is the wife of Richard Vinter, who lives at the cottage on the edge of the golf course. She lives about five miles away at Panstead. She wanted to talk to my husband. I told her that he hadn't returned from town. I asked her if I could take a message. She said she was sorry but she must speak to him, that it was important."

Gringall said: "Had you any idea, Mrs. Charlesworth, what she wanted to talk to your husband about?"

She smiled. "Oh yes," she said. "Of course, I knew her husband owed my husband a great deal of money. I thought it was about that."

Gringall said: "Go on, Mrs. Charlesworth."

She continued: "I told Mrs. Vinter that when my husband came in I'd ask him to ring her up. She gave me her telephone number and I wrote it down. When my husband came in I gave him the message. That would be about ten minutes to seven. I told him directly he arrived. He telephoned her from the hall. I went upstairs to my room. After a little while he came up. He told me that Mrs. Vinter had informed him that her husband was going to Canada, that she'd said that if he wanted to get his money he'd better do something about it. He told me too, that she'd warned him that Vinter could be dangerous. She advised him to take care."

Gringall asked: "What did your husband think about that warning?"

Mrs. Charlesworth said sadly: "He didn't take it seriously. He said he'd always known Vinter to be a bluffer, that he was going to call his bluff. He said he was going to see Vinter right away. He went straight out."

Gringall said: "What did you do, Mrs. Charlesworth? You didn't by any chance go with him?"

She said: "No, I stayed here."

Gringall said: "You're quite sure that perhaps a few minutes afterwards you didn't decide that you wanted to speak to your husband? You didn't by any chance go after him?"

She said: "No. Why should I?"

Gringall said: "Forgive a question which might sound a little unpleasant, Mrs. Charlesworth. But are you sure you've told us all the conversation that your husband said he had with Mrs. Vinter?"

She looked surprised. She said in an odd sort of voice: "I don't know what you mean."

Gringall said: "I'll explain. Are you sure, Mrs. Charlesworth, that your husband didn't tell you that in addition to the other things Mrs. Vinter said, she also suggested to him that you might be leaving the country with Vinter?"

Mrs. Charlesworth got up. She presented a picture of outraged dignity. Callaghan thought she would have made a good actress.

She said: "What you suggest, Mr. Gringall, is absolutely untrue."

Gringall said: "I'm sorry if I've annoyed you, Mrs. Charlesworth. There are one or two other questions I'd like to ask you. I don't think you'll find them at all annoying."

Callaghan got up. He said: "Gringall, I'm expecting to meet Nikolls at the Peacock. He might have some information for me. If you don't mind I'll get along. I'll come back here and pick you up."

Gringall said: "All right. I'll wait for you."

Callaghan went out of the drawing-room. He stood for a minute in the hallway. The sight of the telephone reminded him of something. He went over to the telephone table, looked for a moment at the telephone pad, then he shrugged his shoulders. He went out.

He began to walk slowly down the road towards Vinter's cottage.

Nikolls was drinking a double whisky and soda at the Peacock. Callaghan went to the bar, lit a cigarette. He said: "Well, any news, Windy?"

Nikolls said: "You bet. It's in the bag. You've earned that five hundred from Vinter all right."

Callaghan said: "What is it?"

Nikolls said: "Vinter's got a cut and dried alibi, and nothing can shake it. Charlesworth was shot about ten minutes past seven. Well, Vinter said he was walking round the golf course at that time."

Callaghan said: "I know that's what he says."

Nikolls grinned. "The joke is, that's the truth," he said. "The greenkeeper of the golf club was working at the eleventh green right on the other side of the golf course at five past seven. He saw Vinter walking past. He passed him within about ten yards. It would have been impossible for Vinter to have been anywhere near the place where Charlesworth was shot in that time. That lets him out."

Callaghan said: "Well, I'm not surprised."

Nikolls said: "What do you mean, you're not surprised!"

Callaghan picked up his hat. He said: "Come along with me. You'll see why."

A neat maid let Callaghan and Nikolls into the Charlesworth house. They went into the drawing-room. Gringall was busy making notes.

Callaghan said: "I think I can save you some trouble, Gringall. Vinter didn't kill Charlesworth."

Gringall said: "What do you mean?"

Callaghan said: "He's got an alibi—a good one. He was seen by the greenkeeper at the eleventh hole on the golf course at five past seven. That lets him out."

Mrs. Charlesworth said: "But that's ridiculous. He must have killed my husband."

Callaghan said: "Oh no, he didn't."

She said: "What do you mean?" Her voice was angry.

Callaghan said: "Your husband was killed by Mrs. Vinter, Mrs. Charlesworth. The whole thing was a frame-up between herself and her husband. He was going to Canada with your husband's money, and she was going with him. The fact that they'd been living apart for the last six months made a marvelous set-up for them. You see, when she rang you up just before your husband returned she knew he wasn't in."

Gringall said: "How could she know that?"

Callaghan said: "Because she was waiting in the A.A. telephone box down the road. She could see the house from there. She asked Mrs. Charlesworth to get her husband to ring her up when he came in. She gave Mrs. Charlesworth the number. That number's still on the telephone pad outside in the hall, but it wasn't the number of Mrs. Vinter's house—five miles away. It was the number of the A.A. box down the road where she was waiting for Charlesworth as he went past."

Gringall whistled between his teeth.

Callaghan said: "It was a nice idea. Mrs. Vinter warns Charlesworth that her husband's going to shoot him. She tells Charlesworth that his wife's going off with Vinter. She and her husband know that he is going to be suspected, so they also arrange that he has a perfect alibi, and nobody is going to suspect her."

Gringall picked up his hat. He said: "I think we'll go and see Mrs. Vinter. It was lucky you looked at that telephone pad in the hall, Callaghan."

Callaghan said: "That wouldn't have helped. What was lucky was that when I saw Mrs. Vinter this afternoon I asked to use her telephone. *I remembered the number.*"

3

THEY KIDNAPPED CECILIA

Mrs. Caradine handed Callaghan the unsigned, hand-printed note. He read it:

We have got your ward Cecilia and if you want to see her again you'd better get £25,000 in fivers and tenners from the bank and be ready to hand it over when we tell you.

If you go to the pleece or try any funny bisness little Cecilia will get her throte cut so now you know.

If you're going to play ball put this advertisement in the Daily Echo *personal colum Thursday morning—'Cecilia O.K. as arranged.' Remember no pleece no funny bisness otherwise she gets the werks.*

Callaghan looked at Mrs. Caradine. She was about forty-five, pretty, intelligent, unhappy. He felt sorry for her. He said: "What am I to do about this, Mrs. Caradine?"

She said tearfully: "I've come to you because I think I'd like you to be the person to pay over the money."

Callaghan said: "So you're going to pay?"

She looked at him piteously. "What else can I do?" she asked. "That note might be sheer bluff. On the other hand they might mean what they say. After all, Cecilia is going to be the owner of a considerable estate when she reaches the age of twenty-five in three weeks' time. It would be terrible if we didn't pay the money and these horrible people carried out their threat and killed her."

Callaghan nodded. He said: "That's true enough." He lit a cigarette. "Tell me something, Mrs. Caradine—

something about yourself and Cecilia. Give me a picture. Tell me if she had any lovers—anybody who is likely to be concerned in this."

She said: "I'm a widow, Mr. Callaghan. My husband died ten years ago. When he died his guardianship of Cecilia devolved on me. I became her sole trustee. She comes into her money in three weeks' time when she's twenty-five years of age."

Callaghan asked: "Was she interested in any man?"

"Yes," said Mrs. Caradine. "Two years ago she met a young man—a strange young man called Eugene Rimley—rather an odd type. She wanted to be engaged to him. I didn't like him and I refused my consent. A year ago I altered my mind. I thought I hadn't been wise in refusing. So I consented to an understanding between the two of them that they could be engaged on Cecilia's twenty-fifth birthday."

Callaghan said: "Well, that didn't do much good, did it? She'll come into her money on her twenty-fifth birthday and she can marry whom she likes."

She nodded. "I know. But my idea was that if I held out the hope that I would give my sanction at the end of the year, it would at least give them a year to get tired of each other."

"I see," said Callaghan. "So it doesn't look as if this Eugene Rimley would have anything to do with the kidnapping. He'd have no motive. Do you know where he lives?"

"Yes," said Mrs. Caradine. "He has an apartment at Lanchester Mansions in Pelmayne Square."

Callaghan said: "All right. Now what do you want me to do about this, Mrs. Caradine?"

She said: "The first thing I want to do is to get Cecilia back. I'm going to draw the twenty-five thousand pounds and hand it over to you. I'm going to ask you to put that advertisement in the Daily Echo. Then when the instructions come as to how this money is to be paid over I'm going to get you to pay it over."

"Very well, Mrs. Caradine, we'll do what you suggest," said Callaghan. He shrugged his shoulders. "I don't see that we can do anything else. We'll put this advertisement in the *Daily Echo* personal column on Thursday morning: *'Cecilia O.K. as arranged.'* Then Mrs. Caradine, I imagine you'll receive another communication from these people. Directly you hear from them where, when and how the money is to be handed over, you'd better let me know."

She said: "Very well, Mr. Callaghan." She got up. "Thank you very much," she said. "I do hope everything's going to be all right."

"So do I," said Callaghan.

Nikolls came in at one o'clock. He said to Callaghan: "Effie said you wanted me. What's cookin' around here?"

Callaghan said: "Believe it or not a girl named Cecilia Grant's been kidnapped. Her guardian—a Mrs. Caradine—has been in this morning to see us about it. The kidnappers want twenty-five thousand pounds. They're going to give us instructions as to how and where to pay it over. Our business is to pay the money and hope the girl's returned."

Nikolls said: "Sounds like Chicago in nineteen thirty-five. Is this England or am I dreamin'?"

Callaghan said: "You're probably dreaming. But that's how it is."

Nikolls produced a box of cigarettes. He extracted one with his teeth, struck a match on the seat of his trousers expertly.

He said: "Well, where do I go from here?"

Callaghan said: "There's a fellow called Eugene Rimley. This boyo has been keen on Cecilia for a couple of years. He wants to marry her. At first Mrs. Caradine wouldn't give her consent, but last year, after thinking it over, she changed her mind and said she'd consent to an engagement after a year. She did this to stop them doing anything funny in the meantime—such as running away. It looks as if Rimley has nothing to do with this business, because in any event the girl comes into her money in three weeks' time, so if Rimley wanted to get at that he'd get it by marrying her. He doesn't have to kidnap her. But I'm curious about him. I got his address from Mrs. Caradine. Here it is. You go out and find out what you can about Eugene Rimley. Get his background, talk to him if you like."

Nikolls yawned. He said: "O.K." He went out.

Callaghan was finishing his second whisky and soda in the subterranean Owl's Club when Nikolls came in. He said: "What about Rimley?"

"Rimley looks O.K.," said Nikolls. "He says he's worried sick about Cecilia. On the night she was kidnapped he'd gotta date to take her to the movies, but he was workin'

late in his office—he works for a firm of motor manu-
facturers. He rang through to Mrs. Caradine's house in
the evenin' and said he wouldn't be able to meet Cecilia
because he'd gotta work late. That was true. He did work
at the office till eleven o'clock that night."

Callaghan said: "I see. What about Cecilia?"

"When he rang through to the house," Nikolls went on,
"she'd already left. Nobody's seen her since then. Anyhow,
I don't see this guy's gotta motive for knockin' the girl
off. He's got nothin' to gain by it an' everythin' to lose."

Callaghan nodded. He said: "Well, something may
turn up."

Mrs. Caradine came through on the telephone at five-
thirty on Thursday evening. She said to Callaghan: "Mr.
Callaghan, there's been a phone call ten minutes ago
about Cecilia. He sounded uneducated and nasty. He
said they'd seen the advertisement in the *Daily Echo*,
that the twenty-five thousand pounds was to be put into
a leather attaché case, and whoever was going to deliver
the money was to take a train—not a car—to-morrow
night, Friday, to Epsom, he was to walk half a mile along
the Downs road till he came to the Roebuck Inn, take the
bridle-path on the left of the road twenty-five yards pm:
the Roebuck Inn, walk down this path until he came to
the coppice two hundred yards down. He was to turn
into this coppice. In the middle of the coppice is a little
clearing. In this clearing, standing by itself, is an oak
tree with a hollow trunk. The attaché case containing
the money is to be put into the hollow trunk of the tree."

Callaghan said: "I see."

"The man said that if this is done Cecilia will be home by five o'clock on Saturday morning," Mrs. Caradine went on. "He said that if there's any funny business, or if they see anything to make them at all suspicious, they will kill Cecilia without a moment's hesitation. He sounded as if he meant it," she added miserably.

Callaghan said-: "All right, Mrs. Caradine. I'll do the job myself to-morrow night. Can you arrange for the money to be here some time to-morrow afternoon?"

She said: "Yes, I'll get it from the bank to-morrow. I'll bring it myself."

Callaghan stood in front of his office fireplace, smoking. Nikolls, slumped back in the leather armchair, his feet on Callaghan's desk, his soft hat tilted over his nose, said:

"Well, it's a nice racket—twenty-five thousand pounds for nothin'. These guys have got nerve to get away with this. I think they're good."

Callaghan said: "You don't like the idea of paying up, Windy?"

Nikolls said: "I do not. The idea of you walkin' around Epsom with twenty-five thousand smackers in a leather ease, stickin' it in some hollow oak-tree for some mug to swipe up, just makes me so tired you'd hardly believe. That's one thing I don't like . . ."

Callaghan said: "What's the other?"

Nikolls said: "You're takin' this thing too easy. It's not like you to fall for a job like this without puttin' up a show."

Callaghan said: "Let's wait and see. But I tell you what you might do. Get out and see if you can find Blooey

Stevens. You'll find him at the Metropole Club if I know anything—that place in Seven Dials. You remember Blooey?"

Nikolls said: "Do I! He hasn't been out long, the last stretch they gave him was a nice one. Ten years, wasn't it?"

"Seven and a half," said Callaghan. "He's got two years and a half off for good behaviour."

Nikolls said: "O.K. What do I do? Bring him in by force?"

Callaghan said: "You won't have to. Give him a couple of drinks and tell him there's a fiver in it. He'll come."

Nikolls said: "O.K." He took his feet off the desk. "Anything fresh about Rimley?" asked Callaghan.

"Nothing much," said Nikolls. "But he's got himself a coupla steamship tickets. He ordered them this mornin'."

Callaghan said: "I see. Where does he think he's going?"

Nikolls said: "He thinks he's goin' to Lisbon. He's goin' in a big way too—first class state-rooms an' everythin' de luxe. Does it mean anythin'?"

Callaghan said: "How do I know?"

It was three o'clock in the morning, dark and raining, when Callaghan let himself into his office.

Nikolls was sitting at his desk drinking coffee made on the electric heater. He said: "Hello, Slim. Did you find the oak-tree? Did you leave the money?"

Callaghan nodded. "Yes," he nodded. "Any news?"

Nikolls shook his head. Callaghan sat down. He lit a cigarette, took the cup of coffee that Nikolls handed him.

At four o'clock the telephone jangled. It was Mrs. Caradine.

She said joyfully: "Mr. Callaghan, it's all right. Cecilia arrived home ten minutes ago. She's perfectly all right. She's got a most amazing story to tell. When she went out to keep that movie appointment with Eugene, somebody came up behind her, put his hands over her eyes, and before she knew where she was she was pushed into a car of some sort, blindfolded and taken away. Apparently she was dropped a quarter of an hour ago, again blindfolded, in a car, not a hundred yards from this house. She took the bandage off her eyes and came home at once. She seems none the worse for her experience."

Callaghan said: "A pretty expensive one, though, Mrs. Caradine. It's cost twenty-five thousand pounds. I'll come along and see you sometime."

She said: "Do, Mr. Callaghan. We can never thank you enough for what you've done."

Callaghan hung up. He said to Nikolls: "Get through to Rimley at his private address, keep on ringing until he answers the telephone. I want to talk to him."

Four minutes afterwards Nikolls handed him the receiver.

Callaghan said: "Is that you, Rimley? My name's Callaghan. I'm a private detective. I was employed by Mrs. Caradine to hand over that ransom money for Cecilia. You'll be glad to hear she's returned home safely. She's all right."

Rimley said: "I'm very glad to hear it."

Callaghan said: "Rimley, a little bird tells me that you're leaving for Lisbon in a few days. Are you taking Cecilia with you?"

Rimley said: "Not on your life. Do you think I'd marry that girl after everyone has been snooping around the place, practically suggesting all the time that I had something to do with this kidnapping? I'm fed up with it. Right from the start Mrs. Caradine has suggested that my idea in marrying Cecilia was simply to get her money. Now you can tell her that I don't intend to marry Cecilia. They can find somebody more worthy of her."

Callaghan said: "I see. I suppose it would be unfair to suggest that you'd changed your mind because Cecilia's estate is going to be minus the twenty-five thousand pounds paid for this kidnapping thing?"

Rimley said: "You know what you can do with your suggestions."

Callaghan hung up.

The morning sun came through the big French windows of the Caradine drawing-room.

Mrs. Caradine said: "Cecilia, this is Mr. Callaghan—the detective who paid over the kidnap money."

Callaghan shook hands. He said: "Miss Grant, why don't you tell the truth about this kidnapping business? Why don't you save a lot of bother and admit that it was a put up job between Rimley and yourself?"

Cecilia Grant said coldly: "Mr. Callaghan, I don't know what you mean."

Callaghan said: "I think you do. You know perfectly well that your guardian, Mrs. Caradine here, had only consented to your being engaged to Rimley after a year in order to stop you two doing something funny. Maybe you or Rimley thought that she'd still try and stop you marrying him, so you wanted to make certain that you could do it. This way you knew you'd get your hands on twenty-five thousand pounds immediately. Well, is that a good guess?"

She said: "No, it isn't, Mr. Callaghan. I—"

Callaghan held up his hand. "Wait a minute," he said. "Perhaps I can tell you something that will alter your opinion. It might interest you to know that now that Rimley has got the twenty-five thousand pounds he's walking out on you."

Cecilia's jaw sagged. She looked at Callaghan blankly.

Callaghan said: "I've been keeping tabs on Rimley for the last three or four days. I wanted him to know he was being watched. He's booked a passage to Lisbon. I rang him up soon after you returned early this morning and told him you were back again. He wasn't even interested. He told me he was so fed up about being suspected in this matter that he was walking out on you. He's going to Lisbon and he's not going alone. Well, what about it, Cecilia?"

Cecilia said: "The swine! So he is lousy after all. You're quite right, Mr. Callaghan—it was a put up job. We arranged it together. I was to pretend to be kidnapped. He was to send the notes. He knew that Mrs. Caradine would fall for it and pay over the money, that she'd never take a chance on anything happening to me. He said we were certain of being able to get married at once. *He's* got that money."

Callaghan said: "It'll be a tough thing for you to get it back. That money's your money, Cecilia. You were an accessory to this kidnapping business—you allowed yourself to be kidnapped. You practically made a gift of this money to this man."

Cecilia said: "How fearful. What an unutterable rotter. What am I to do?"

Mrs. Caradine said wryly: "I don't see what you can do, my dear, except thank your lucky stars that Eugene Rimley has shown his hand. It would have been very much worse if you'd waited a month and married him. What a charming husband he would have made."

Callaghan said: "You're going to pay dearly for your indiscretion, Cecilia." He grinned. "It's cost you twenty-five thousand pounds unless—"

"Unless what?" Cecilia asked.

"Unless you can persuade Mrs. Caradine to do something about it," said Callaghan.

Mrs. Caradine said in a strained voice: "Whatever do you mean, Mr. Callaghan?"

Callaghan said: "I mean you're in this with Rimley, Mrs. Caradine." He turned to Cecilia.

"Listen, Cecilia," he said. "When this fellow Rimley turned up in the first place your guardian Mrs. Caradine wouldn't allow you to have anything to do with him. She didn't like him. All right. A year afterwards she changed her mind. She said she'd give her consent to you two people getting engaged in a year's time—that is just when you're on the point of coming into your inheritance. Then just before the time comes when you do come into possession of your money you're kidnapped. Quite obviously, the people who kidnapped you knew that you had an appointment with Rimley. Obviously whoever kidnapped you was in possession of knowledge that only you and he had."

Callaghan stopped talking, lit a cigarette. Cecilia said nothing.

"But Rimley's behaviour is strange," Callaghan went on. "Very strange. Isn't it? If he'd waited a few weeks he could have married you and had all your money. Not just twenty-five thousand pounds—*unless* he thought that there wasn't going to be any more money!"

Cecilia said in a strange voice: "What do you mean by that?"

"I mean," said Callaghan, "that it looks to me as if Mrs. Caradine has been robbing your estate. She knew there'd been a show-down on your twenty-fifth birthday. She knew Rimley was no good, so she fixed this up with him. He's got the twenty-five thousand pounds from the estate, he doesn't marry you, and if I'm not mistaken, Mrs. Caradine is the person who's going to occupy the other state-room on the Lisbon voyage in a few days."

Cecilia said to Mrs. Caradine: "I don't like the sound of all this, Evelyn. Are you sure you haven't been tampering with my money?"

Mrs. Caradine said: "Well, my dear, I may have used a little here and there."

Callaghan grinned. He said: "You're telling me!"

Cecilia said: "This doesn't look so good, does it, Mr. Callaghan? What am I to do?"

Callaghan said: "Don't worry. Rimley won't get far. We'll have him picked up."

Mrs. Caradine said triumphantly: "If you allow that, Cecilia, you'll never see a penny of your money back anyway. You may as well know now that the twenty-five thousand pounds was the last money in the estate. The best thing for you to do is to come to some arrangement with us. Eugene and I have got that money. We've been found out. It's unlucky, but what can you do about it? You were party to the kidnapping plot yourself."

Callaghan said: "You're making one mistake, Mrs. Caradine. You haven't got the money."

She said: "What do you mean?"

Callaghan said: "I've got the money. The twenty-five thousand pounds that I left in the oak tree was very nice counterfeit provided by my friend Blooey Stevens, the best forger in this country. I knew that whoever examined that attaché case would do it by flashlight in the dark before giving the O.K. to Cecilia to go back home. I knew they wouldn't look carefully, and those notes were very good forgeries."

Cecilia said: "I owe you a lot, Mr. Callaghan."

He grinned at her.

"I'll send my bill in to you," he said. "Good-day, Mrs. Caradine. I hope you enjoy the trip."

4
THE DISAPPEARING DIAMONDS

CALLAGHAN was sitting at the desk in his office when Effie Thompson came in. She said: "Mr. Vanning is here, Mr. Callaghan."

Callaghan said: "All right, Effie. Show him in."

Vanning, a tall thin man with a worried expression on his good-looking face, came into the office. Callaghan said: "Good morning, Mr. Vanning. This is Windemere Nikolls—my Canadian assistant."

"I'm glad to meet you, Mr. Nikolls."

"Yeah, me too . . ." said Nikolls.

Callaghan motioned Vanning to a chair. "What can we do for you, Mr. Vanning?" he asked.

Vanning said: "Mr. Callaghan, yesterday an extraordinary thing happened at my house. A diamond plaque, valued at twenty thousand pounds, disappeared into thin air."

Callaghan smiled. "Diamonds don't disappear into thin air, Mr. Vanning," he said. "Tell me exactly what happened."

Vanning said: "Yesterday morning I was at work in the library. I was doing my accounts. When I opened the safe I saw the case with the diamond plaque in its usual place. I looked at the plaque, closed the case, put it back in the safe. When I'd finished work I handed my account books to my wife, who put them back into the safe and closed the door. Ten minutes after that, at eleven thirty-five precisely, I left the house, I returned at a quarter past twelve. I went to the safe and the plaque had disappeared."

"I see," said Callaghan. He thought for a moment. "Who else left your house yesterday morning," he asked, "between the time that you went out at eleven thirty-five and the time you came back?"

"One person only," said Vanning. "An interior decorator by the name of Charles Francis, a young man who is going to do some work inside the house. He was measuring up the library. My wife tells me that he left about ten minutes after I did."

Callaghan said: "So Mr. Francis had been in the library alone for ten minutes. Is that right?"

"Yes," said Vanning. "That's right."

Nikolls said: "Say, listen. It's a pip! Francis pinched the plaque."

"Shut up, Windy," said Callaghan. "Mr. Vanning, when you returned, opened the safe and found the plaque had disappeared, what did you do?"

"I told my wife. She informed me that nobody with the exception of Francis had left the house."

"And what do you know about Francis?" asked Callaghan. "Has he worked for you before?"

Vanning hesitated. "Well, no . . ." he said. "As a matter of fact it's the first job Francis has done for me. He was going to re-decorate the library. It was my wife's suggestion. You see, she knew Francis at one time or other, He was a friend of hers."

"I see," said Callaghan. He stubbed out his cigarette in the ashtray on the desk. He went on: "Mr. Vanning, don't you think that this is a job for the police? All the evidence seems to point in one direction, doesn't it?"

"Well, I suppose it looks like that," said Vanning. "But I had another idea."

Callaghan raised his eyebrows. "Yes?" he queried.

Vanning said: "I told you the plaque was worth twenty thousand pounds. But I doubt if it would be worth that to anyone who stole it. It would have to be broken up and the diamonds in it would probably have to be re-set. By the time that was done the plaque would have depreciated in value."

"Quite," said Callaghan. "You mean whoever stole it wouldn't be able to get twenty thousand pounds for it?"

"That's what I mean," said Vanning. "So I have thought of another way out of this. I've brought with me three thousand pounds in cash, Mr. Callaghan. I'm going to leave it with you. If you can get the plaque back again by paying over that money and no questions asked, I think possibly that would be the easiest way out of the difficulty."

Callaghan said nothing.

Vanning went on quickly: "I think that would be better than making a lot of bother and possibly not getting the plaque back at all." He took a wallet from the breast pocket of his coat, extracted some banknotes, laid them on the desk in front of him.

Callaghan said: "All right, Mr. Vanning. I'll have the three thousand pounds. I'll see what I can do. What is your telephone number?"

"Kensington 17654," replied Vanning. "I take it you'll telephone me, Mr. Callaghan?"

"Yes," said Callaghan. "Tell me something," he went on. "Who was in your house yesterday morning besides yourself, Mrs. Vanning and Francis?"

Vanning said: "The cook—Mrs. Thwaites, and a housemaid, Eliza Parkes. There was no one else."

"And you left the house at eleven thirty-five exactly?" asked Callaghan.

Vanning nodded.

"Had you any special reason for noticing the time?" Callaghan went on.

"No," said Vanning. "But I'll tell you how I knew the time. Just after I left the house, on the other side of the road, somebody asked me what the time was. I looked at my watch. It was just eleven thirty-five. That's how I knew."

Callaghan said: "All right, Mr. Vanning. We'll see what we can do." He rang the bell on the desk. When Effie Thompson came in, he said "Effie, show Mr. Vanning out, please. And give him a receipt for three thousand pounds."

Effie said: "Very well, Mr. Callaghan."

"Thank you very much," said Vanning. "I knew I was right to come to you. Good morning, Mr. Callaghan."

Callaghan said good morning.

When the door closed behind Vanning he leaned back in his chair. He sighed.

Nikolls said: "Well, what do you know about that one? It's easy, hey?"

"Is it?" asked Callaghan. "What's your idea, Windy?" He took a cigarette from the box on the desk, lit it.

"It's stickin' outa foot," said Nikolls. "The wife, Mrs. Vanning, used to know the interior decorator, Francis.

Maybe he's an old boy friend of hers. She gets him the job to do over the library. He comes along and directly Vanning goes out he opens the safe, pinches the plaque and scrams. As easy as stealin' a sleepin' baby's false teeth!"

Callaghan said: "Yes, It looks too easy to me."

"Well, it's stickin' outa mile," said Nikolls. "Vanning suspects Francis."

"You think so?" asked Callaghan.

"Sure he does. But he don't want any publicity, see? He don't want a stink about it. He don't want anybody to get wise to his wife. So he comes along here, gives you the works, leaves you three thousand quid. The idea bein' that you get around an' try an' buy back the plaque with no questions asked."

"Maybe," said Callaghan. He called: "Effie, get me Kensington 17654."

"Vanning won't be back yet," said Nikolls.

"I want to talk to Mrs. Vanning," said Callaghan. "I'm going to suggest she meets me to-night at the Blue Jay Club."

"Well, for cryin' out loud," said Nikolls. "What's the idea?"

Callaghan said: "There's nothing like the truth, Windy. Everything points to the interior decorator, Francis, having pulled this job. All right, he's an old friend of Mrs. Vanning's. If she's worried about the situation she'll agree to meet me to-night to discuss it. The fact that she agrees to do so will show me that she is worried, that she's worried about Francis."

"Yeah," said Nikolls. "Maybe she's still in love with this mug Francis. *Cherchez la femme!* That's what I always say."

Callaghan said: "Listen, Windy. You get out and do a little snooping. Find out everything you can about the Vanning household. About Vanning, Mrs. Vanning, the cook and the housemaid."

"O.K.," said Nikolls. "Maybe I'll be lucky. Maybe I'll get the dope. I'll try my sex appeal on the housemaid."

"All right," said Callaghan. "But don't try too hard."

Nikolls went out of the office. The telephone jangled. Callaghan lifted the receiver. He asked to speak to Mrs. Vanning.

At eight o'clock that evening Callaghan and Mrs. Vanning were sitting in the lounge at the Blue Jay Club.

Callaghan said: "Now, Mrs. Vanning, about this diamond plaque that was stolen from the library safe at your house yesterday morning. I understand the only person who left the house during your husband's absence was Mr. Francis, the interior decorator. I understand Mr. Francis was a friend of yours, that it was through you he got the job of re-decorating the library."

"Yes," said Mrs. Vanning. "That's the trouble. That's why I wanted to see you, Mr. Callaghan. I'm afraid it's the old, old story."

"Really?" said Callaghan. "And what is the old, old story?" He offered her a cigarette, took one himself.

When he had lit them, Mrs. Vanning said: "Three years ago I thought I was in love with Charles Francis. That was before I met my husband. I thought I was very much in love. Of course I wasn't. Well, when the opportunity came for him to do this work I thought I'd like him to have the chance. He's just started in business for himself. But I've been a fool, Mr. Callaghan. I'm perfectly certain that he stole that plaque. I'm certain that he stole it because he knows I can't very well accuse him of it."

"Why not?" asked Callaghan. "Are you afraid of a spot of blackmail, Mrs. Vanning?"

"To tell you the truth I am."

"How can he blackmail you?" Callaghan went on. "You thought you were in love with him years ago. You discovered you weren't. What is there in that?"

"There's nothing in that, Mr. Callaghan. Nothing at all. But unfortunately, since I've been married I've written him one or two rather foolish letters."

"I see," said Callaghan. "And you think if we bring an accusation of theft against Francis, he's going to threaten to produce those letters, and you think your husband wouldn't like that?"

"He'd loathe it," said Mrs. Vanning. "Heaven knows what he'd do."

Callaghan asked: "Well, have you any suggestion, Mrs. Vanning?"

She thought for a moment, then she said: "I think if someone offered Francis some money he'd listen to reason. I think he'd be afraid to try to dispose of that plaque. If we offered him some money I think he'd return it."

"You really think he'd do that?" Callaghan asked.

"Yes, I'm certain he would. He's always terribly hard up. He's always wanting money."

"Well," said Callaghan, "we might try."

"But where's the money coming from?" asked Mrs. Vanning.

Callaghan smiled. "Luckily for you, Mrs. Vanning," he said, "your husband doesn't want a great deal of publicity, he wants the plaque returned. He gave me three thousand pounds. He told me I was entitled to use that money in getting the plaque returned with no questions asked. Now if what you say is right, and Francis has that plaque and is prepared to listen to reason, for three thousand pounds he might be prepared to return it and those letters."

Mrs. Vanning said: "I know he would, Mr. Callaghan. I'm certain of that."

"Well, it's simple, isn't it?" said Callaghan. "I'll go and see Francis. I'll make him the offer."

"Yes, but . . ." Mrs. Vanning hesitated.

"But what?" asked Callaghan.

"He's a strange person," she went on. "He might suspect. He might think it was a trap. Wouldn't it be better . . .?" She paused.

Callaghan asked: "Wouldn't what be better?"

"Mr. Callaghan, if I went to see Francis . . . if I took the three thousand pounds, I think he'd return the plaque and the letters to me. I can hand the plaque back to you. You could say that you'd been able to get it through your own underworld connections. My husband need never know. Everything would be all right. Mr. Callaghan, please."

Callaghan thought for a moment. "Well, it might work," he said.

"I'm certain it would," said Mrs. Vanning, "especially if you mark those notes."

Callaghan raised his eyebrows. "Why, Mrs. Vanning?"

"If you mark the notes we should have proof that they'd been paid to Francis. He couldn't blackmail me again afterwards. You see, he'd have to pay the notes into a banking account or change them somewhere, and if they were marked so that he couldn't see . . ."

Callaghan said: "That's a good idea. We'd have him then in any event. We'd be able to prove that he'd accepted those notes." He got up. "Look, Mrs. Vanning," he went on, "I suggest that we get a cab and go back to my office. I'll mark those notes, hand them over to you. Then you can get in touch with Francis, give him the marked notes, get the plaque and the letters, return the plaque to me. And don't worry. I'll straighten everything out. Your husband need never know anything about it."

It was ten o'clock the following morning when Callaghan came into the office. Nikolls was sitting on Effie Thompson's desk reading the paper. He followed Callaghan into his office. Callaghan said: "Well, Windy, what have you got?"

Nikolls sighed. "I spent a whole lotta time on this business last night," he said. "That housemaid at Vanning's place is no ordinary housemaid."

Callaghan asked: "What did she know?"

"Plenty," said Nikolls. "First of all she gave me a tip about this Francis guy, the interior decorator. It looks like this mug ain't any good. Three or four days ago, Eliza—that's the housemaid—listened in on the telephone extension line when Mrs. Vannin' was talkin' to him, see? She was talkin' about the interior decoratin' that this Francis is supposed to do, but he wasn't interested."

"No?" said Callaghan. "What was he interested in?"

Nikolls said: "Well, the housemaid baby reckons that he was tryin' 'to work the black' on the Vannin dame. She heard him tell her that he wanted the money an' he was gonna have it—one way or the other. He said that if she didn't cash in good an' quick he was comin' around to see Vannin' an' that when he did come around he was goin' to bring her letters with him."

Callaghan asked: "Well . . . what did she say to that?"

"She told him to lay off . . . she said if he'd be patient she'd fix it somehow. An' I reckon she fixed it all right. She couldn't give him the dough so she let him get at the diamonds. That's my theory."

Callaghan nodded. He took his cigarette case from his pocket, lit a cigarette. "What else?" he asked.

Nikolls went on: "What Vannin' told you was O.K. Francis was in the library when Vannin' left. Mrs. Vannin' went to the door an' saw Vannin' off an' then she went straight to her room. Francis left the house about ten minutes afterwards—about eleven forty-five. An' that stuff that Vannin' told you about him leavin' at eleven thirty-five an' knowin' that was the time because he looked at his watch when some guy asked him is O.K."

"How do you know that, Windy?" Callaghan asked.

"I checked with the hall-porter—the guy on the door of the apartment house opposite. He saw Vannin' come out an' just as he crossed the road a guy who lives in the apartment house—Velazy his name is—was just goin' out. He stopped Vannin' and asked him the time. Vannin' told him—eleven thirty-five."

"I see," said Callaghan. "Did you find out anything else about the Vannings?"

Nikolls said: "Yeah, I found out somethin' about her. She used to be on the music-halls in a magicians' act an' who do you think her partner was? It was nobody else but the guy Velazy, the guy who asked Vannin' the time."

Callaghan whistled. "Did she know Francis then?" he asked.

"Sure she did," said Nikolls. "She met Francis when she was on the halls. The Velazy Magical Duo they usta call the act. An' she was supposed to be engaged to Francis. Then Vannin' turned up an' she took a run-out on Francis an' married Vannin'. This case is easy. This guy Francis has got somethin' on her. He's been blackmailing her. When he found she hadn't got any dough he had the diamonds instead."

The telephone jangled. Callaghan took off the receiver. It was Mrs. Vanning. She said: "Mr. Callaghan, I've been in touch with Francis. I've arranged to see him at seven o'clock this evening. I suggest I meet you at the Blue Jay Club at eight-thirty afterwards. Then I can tell you What's happened. Is that all right?"

Callaghan said: "That's perfectly all right, Mrs. Vanning." He hung up, turned to Nikolls. He said: "By the way, Windy, do you happen to know the apartment number of this Velazy fellow who asked Vanning the time—Mrs. Vanning's one-time music-hall partner?"

"Yeah," said Nikolls. "The hall-porter told me he lives at No. 14 on the first floor. He said he was a nice guy. Why, what's the big idea?"

Callaghan said: "Oh nothing—nothing much. But I've got an idea in my head. I'd like to have a little talk with Velazy. He might be able to tell me something. You never know."

"Well, I hope it keeps fine for you," said Nikolls.

Callaghan stubbed out his cigarette, put on his hat and went out.

Mrs. Vanning was waiting in the lounge at the Blue Jay Club when Callaghan went in. Her face was pale. She looked very worried.

Callaghan said: "Good evening, Mrs. Vanning. Why, what's the matter? You look as if you've seen a ghost. What's wrong?"

Mrs. Vanning said: "It's Francis. I've seen him. Mr. Callaghan, he was beastly. Thank heaven we marked those notes."

"I see," said Callaghan. "So he pulled a fast one on you, Mrs. Vanning. He took the notes and refused to hand over the diamond plaque or the letters, hey?"

"Yes. Isn't it terrible?" Her voice trembled.

Callaghan said: "I wonder how I'm going to account to your husband for that three thousand pounds. He'll think I'm a hell of a detective, won't he?"

She nodded. She said: "It's terrible. Well . . . there's only one thing to be done."

"What's that?" asked Callaghan.

"I must tell my husband the whole story. We must go to the police."

"Oh no, Mrs. Vanning," said Callaghan. "It isn't necessary." His voice had changed. It was cold, incisive.

Mrs. Vanning looked surprised. "What do you mean?" she said.

Callaghan said: "I've got the diamond plaque, so there's nothing to go to the police about."

She gasped. "I don't understand—"

"You wouldn't, would you?" said Callaghan. "Earlier to-day I went round and saw your old-time partner on the music-halls— Velazy. I told him it would be pretty good for his health if he handed over that diamond plaque. I told him just how it got into his possession. Well, he's a reasonable person. He was wise, Mrs. Vanning. He handed it over."

"So you know . . . you know . . .?" she said.

"Yes," said Callaghan. "You know, Mrs. Vanning, all the evidence pointed much too directly against Francis and one thing gave Velazy away. When I went into the apartment house in which he lives I noticed a large electrically controlled clock in the hall. I wondered why it was necessary for Velazy, who must have passed that clock on his way out—he must have seen it—to have to ask your husband the time. Then I got it. You two used to call yourselves the Velazy Magical Duo. Your act was a sleight-of-hand act. You were engaged to Francis. You had money from him. You probably owe him a lot of money. Vanning turned up and you thought he'd make a better match. So you walked out on Francis, walked out on your partner Velazy and married Vanning." Callaghan paused. "Well . . .?" he concluded.

Mrs. Vanning shrugged her shoulders. "Something like that," she admitted.

Callaghan went on: "Recently, Francis began to worry for the money you owed him. Your housemaid overheard a conversation he had with you on the telephone the other day. He said unless you paid he was coming to see your husband and he was going to bring the letters with him. They weren't indiscreet letters you'd written to him, Mrs. Vanning. Obviously they were letters admitting that you owed him the money, saying that you'd try to pay sometime."

"Yes," said Mrs. Vanning. "I did tell him that."

"So then you get a bright idea to get rid of Francis," continued Callaghan. "You suggested to your husband that Francis should be engaged to do the interior decorating in the library. You sent for him to come round on a morning that you knew your husband would be there doing his accounts. The safe door was open. You took your opportunity and when your husband gave you the account books to put away, you removed the diamond plaque from its velvet case and closed the safe door. You knew your husband was going about half past eleven—he had an appointment. And when he went into the hall to go out you slipped the plaque into his overcoat pocket. Well, isn't that right, Mrs. Vanning?"

She nodded.

Callaghan went on: "Velazy was waiting in the doorway of the apartment house opposite. As your husband crossed the road Velazy came out, asked him the time and, whilst your husband was looking at his watch, Velazy picked his pocket. Francis left the house ten minutes later and suspicion must fall on him. Never in a million years would your husband realize that he himself was the person who took the diamond plaque out of the house, that he carried it from you to Velazy."

Mrs. Vanning laughed—a bitter laugh. "You are pretty clever, aren't you, Mr. Callaghan?" she said.

"Too clever for you," said Callaghan. "The next thing you had to do was to build up your case against Francis. So you got me to mark those notes just in case, as you put it, Francis tried to cause any trouble afterwards. In fact, you've given him those notes in part payment of the money you legally owe him. And you thought you'd got him where you wanted him. You're now suggesting that we go to the police and have him arrested. Not a very nice person, are you? And you're in a spot, aren't you . . . a bad spot?"

"Well, that's that," said Mrs. Vanning. "And where do we go from here, Mr. Callaghan?"

"I think we'll go and see your husband," said Callaghan. "And on the way you decide something."

"What?" she asked.

Callaghan said: "Who is going to tell him . . . you or me?"

5
THE TELEPHONE TALKS

CALLAGHAN sat at the corner table in the deserted bar of the Blue Jay Club. His chair was tilted backwards against the wall. In front of him his third whisky and soda stood on the table. He looked up casually as the ponderous form of his assistant, Windemere Nikolls, came through the doorway, threaded its way between the tables.

Callaghan said: "Well, Windy?"

Nikolls sat down on a chair opposite Callaghan. He eyed the whisky and soda enviously. He said: "Look, believe it or not, we got some business."

"No?" said Callaghan. "At eight o'clock at night?"

"Yeah," said Nikolls. "I was just leaving the office an' she comes in. Boy—is she a babe! She's lovely. She's got a skin like grade A milk. She's a blonde—a real one—with the bluest sorta eyes that make you go all funny inside. An' does she know how to dress—"

Callaghan interrupted casually. He said: "She seems a considerable sort of girl. What does she want?"

Nikolls said: "I wouldn't know. But she needs a detective. She wouldn't talk to me. She wants to see you."

Callaghan asked: "Where is she now?"

Nikolls said: "She's gone off some place. She wanted to stick around in the waitin' room, but I wouldn't have that. I said maybe I could put my finger on you, that if I could maybe you'd come back to the office and see her at half past eight. I said she'd better come back then."

Callaghan nodded. He said: "All right."

Nikolls asked: "You gonna see her?"

Callaghan said: "Perhaps. Perhaps not. But you can go off, Windy. Come in at ten o'clock to-morrow morning."

"O.K.," said Nikolls. He went away.

Callaghan drank the whisky and soda slowly. Then he tilted his chair back against the wall again. He looked at his wristwatch. It was five past eight. He got up, put on his black soft hat, went out of the bar.

At twenty past eight, Callaghan unlocked the door of the outer office, crossed the room and entered his private office. He had time to switch on the lights, help himself to a cigarette from the silver box on the table, when the telephone jangled. Callaghan picked it up. A harsh staccato voice said: "Is that Callaghan Investigations?"

Callaghan said: "Yes."

"Are you Callaghan?" asked the voice.

Callaghan said: "I'm Mr. Callaghan. What's your trouble?"

The voice said: "I haven't got any trouble. The trouble's all yours. You've either had a visit, or you're going to have a visit—from my wife—Mrs. Raven. You can't mistake her," the voice continued sarcastically, "she's very beautiful, But my advice to you, Callaghan—or Mister Callaghan if you prefer that—is not to take anything she says too seriously. She has a very vivid imagination. In fact her name ought to be Ananias, not Isobella."

Callaghan said: "Thank you for nothing. Is that all?"

The voice said: "Yes, that's all. I hope it's enough."

Callaghan said amiably: "Thank you for calling through. And nuts to you!"

He hung up the receiver with a jerk just as the outer office door bell rang.

The woman sat in the big leather armchair opposite the desk. Slumped back in his chair, Callaghan looked at her sideways through the haze of cigarette smoke. He thought that Nikolls had been right about her. She was beautiful, exquisitely turned out. Her furs were expensive, and the one hand not hidden by the small muff she carried, was small, white and artistic.

He said: "Well, Mrs. Raven?"

She spread her hands despairingly. Callaghan thought she was very beautiful. And her eyes were piteous—a woman who had been hurt badly, he thought.

She said: "I'm afraid it's the usual story, Mr. Callaghan, with, possibly, a slight variation. I have been married for eighteen months. I married my husband because I was practically forced into it by my people, both of whom have since died. Well, life hasn't been easy."

Callaghan said: "No, married life isn't easy sometimes. That's practically the first thing a private detective learns."

She went on: "I've stuck it as long as I could. Well, two or three months ago something happened."

Callaghan said: "I can guess. You fell in love with somebody else."

She nodded. "I fell in love with somebody else. Can you understand that, Mr. Callaghan?"

Callaghan said: "I can understand most things. All right, so you're in love with another man. Go on, Mrs. Raven."

She said: "My only other friend in the world besides this man is my uncle. Two or three months ago I went to him and told him the whole story. He was sympathetic, but he did not believe it would be a good thing for me to break up my marriage. He believed that if my husband and I went on for a little longer we might straighten out our differences. He said that if we tried it for another six months—if I would promise not to see this man for six months—he would give my husband and myself five thousand pounds each, with which, as he put it, to begin life afresh."

Callaghan said: "I see. Well, is it worth the five thousand pounds you get if you go on living with your husband, Mrs. Raven?"

She said: "No. But I wanted the money, so I agreed. But I'm afraid I've fallen down on the job. I've continued to live with my husband, but I see the man whom I love. Oh, don't think there's anything wrong in it. We just have tea or something like that in a public restaurant. We feel we must see each other."

Callaghan said: "In other words you're trying to have it both ways?"

Her shoulders drooped. She said: "Can't you understand, Mr. Callaghan?"

Callaghan said: "I understand. Well?"

She said: "Mr. Callaghan, my husband is plotting something. I don't know what it is. I'm perfectly certain that he knows nothing of these clandestine meetings, but he suspects. He's a strange, odd man. I don't think he's quite sane. He said the other day that he was perfectly certain I was only staying with him until I got that five thousand pounds, that once I'd got it I'd leave him."

Callaghan said: "He's right, isn't he?"

She said miserably: "Yes. He's right."

Callaghan said: "Well, you can't expect him to like it, can you?"

"No." She shook her head.

He asked: "Mrs. Raven, what's worrying you?"

She said slowly: "This: he said there was one way that he could stop me getting that money—one way."

Callaghan asked: "I wonder what that would be?"

She said: "I believe he's going to commit suicide. I believe that's what he meant. He thinks if he did that I shouldn't get the money."

Callaghan said: "Maybe you're right. He's not awfully fond of you, is he? He doesn't sound an awfully attractive sort of person."

She looked at him. Her cornflower blue eyes wide with amazement. She said: "What do you mean?"

Callaghan said: "He was on the telephone to me a few minutes ago. He said some very uncomplimentary things about you."

She asked tremulously: "And did you believe them?"

Callaghan said: "Now that I've seen you I can't say I do. By the way, how did he know you were coming here?"

She said: "That's my fault, I'm afraid. Two or three days ago a friend of mine mentioned your name. She said you were the best private detective in London, that you were clever and that underneath that very tough exterior you were sometimes kind. To-day I felt quite desperate about things. I made up my mind to telephone you. I went to the telephone in the hall, found your name in the book. Then I heard his key in the lock. I hung up the telephone, went away. But he's very clever, Mr. Callaghan,

I've a habit that a lot of women have of scoring under the name I want to ring with my fingernail. Foolishly when I left the telephone I didn't close the book. There's not the slightest doubt that he looked through the names, found the fingernail mark under your name and put two and two together. He's that sort of man."

Callaghan said: "I see. Well, Mrs. Raven, and what do I do?"

She said pleadingly: "Mr. Callaghan, I want you to keep my husband under observation. I want you to see what he does, where he goes. I'm frightened. Perhaps -I can see you again in a few days and you can tell me what you think?"

Callaghan said: "Do you mean you would like me to go and talk to your husband, Mrs. Raven?"

She said: "If you thought it would do any good. If you would."

"All right," said Callaghan. "What's his address?"

"It's in St. John's Wood," she said. She gave him the address.

Callaghan said: "And the other man—the man you love—where does he live?"

She answered: "His name's Eustace Lyster. He lives in Kensington at 323 Alfred Place. But . . ."

Callaghan said: "It's all right. I shan't bother him. But I like to have all the facts. Come and see me in two or three days' time. Maybe I'll have some news for you."

She said: "Mr. Callaghan, I can't tell you how grateful I am."

He got up. He said: "I shouldn't think your meeting with your husband to-night would be very pleasant."

She said: "I shan't see him. Luckily I'm not going back home. I'd arranged to stay for a few days with a girl friend at Hampstead. My address will be 14 Towers Road."

Callaghan said: "Well, I'm glad of that. Your husband didn't sound too good-natured to me. Good-night, Mrs. Raven."

He showed her to the door.

Somewhere in the neighborhood a clock struck ten. The cold had increased and a slight mist was creeping along the deserted street. Callaghan pushed open the gate of the Raven house in St. John's Wood, walked up the tiled path to the front door. He pressed the bell button, waited. Nothing happened. He stood playing tunes on the bell-push for five minutes, then he took a bunch of keys from his pocket and started work on the door.

Three minutes later he stepped into the hall, closing the door quietly behind him.

A peculiar sense of heat, a rush of warm air, came towards him. At the end of the hallway he could see a gleam of light beneath a door. He crossed the hall, opened the door, stood in the doorway.

The room was small, comfortably furnished. The heat was terrific. A heaped coal fire blazed at one end of the room, at the other an electric fire burned. Slumped beside the armchair in front of the fire was the figure of a man. An automatic pistol lay close to his right hand. The carpet was soaked with blood.

Callaghan crossed the room, stood looking at the body. It seemed as if Raven had carried out his threat.

He went out of the room, across the hall, took the latch off the front door, went out into the street. He walked until he found a telephone box a hundred yards from the house. He called Nikolls. He said: "Listen, Windy, I'm at a house called Templeton just off Acacia Road, St. John's Wood. Get the car and get out here as quickly as you can. Bring a fingerprint outfit with you. Get a move on."

Nikolls said: "O.K."

Callaghan hung up. He went back to the house, stood in front of the fire, moodily smoking. At a quarter to eleven Nikolls said: "If there were any fingerprints on the butt of that gun, I've got 'em. But they'll be his, won't they? He shot himself—look at the powder burns round the wound."

Callaghan said: "Perhaps—perhaps not."

"All right," said Nikolls. "Maybe not. So who else done it—Mrs. Raven's boy friend, hey?"

"Why not?" said Callaghan. "It would be interesting to know what he was doing to-night."

Nikolls scratched his head ruminatively. "What the hell?" he said. "This guy threatened to commit suicide. It looks like a suicide."

"Perhaps it is," said Callaghan. He picked up the automatic pistol with his gloved hand, took out his hand-kerchief, wiped the gun butt.

Nikolls looked at him in amazement. He said: "Look, Slim, what is this—you get me round here to take the prints off this gun and then you clean it up? You know what you're doing—you're destroyin' evidence."

Callaghan said casually: "That's what I thought. Let's go."

They went out of the house.

Down the street Callaghan paused at the call box, went inside. He telephoned Whitehall 1212.

When Scotland Yard answered he asked for the information room. He was put through quickly. He said: "There's a dead man in a ground floor sitting-room at a house called Templeton, just off the Acacia Road, St. John's Wood. I think he's shot himself. I thought you might like to know."

The soft voice of the policewoman on the switchboard said: "Thank you very much. And who are you, please?"

Callaghan said: "Santa Claus." He hung up.

When he came out of the call box, Nikolls said: "Look, if you're right, this boy friend of Mrs. Raven's is a tough egg."

Callaghan said: "He might be. I'll go and see him to-morrow. It would be amusing if he hadn't got an alibi for this evening. And by the way, Windy, I'm a little bit worried about Mrs. Raven. She's staying with a girl friend at 14 Towers Road, Hampstead. Just keep an eye on her for the next day or two. I don't want anything to happen to her."

At eleven o'clock next morning Callaghan went into a sitting-room at 323 Alfred Place, Kensington. Lyster came towards him, his hand outstretched.

"I'm glad to meet you, Mr. Callaghan," he said. "Isobella told me she was going to see you to ask your advice about her husband. I suppose you've come to see me about that."

Callaghan said: "Yes and no. Tell me something, Mr. Lyster. What were you doing last night between half past eight and ten o'clock?"

Lyster said: "Well, I'd made up my mind I was going to have a show-down with Raven. I'd made up my mind I was going to tell him exactly what I thought about him and his treatment of his wife. I walked out to his place in St. John's Wood, but when I got there I changed my mind. I just walked around for a bit and came home."

Callaghan said: "I see. You didn't take an automatic pistol with you, did you?"

"What!" exclaimed Lyster. Then he eyes moved to a desk across the room. He said: "Whatever do you mean?"

Callaghan said: "Raven either shot himself last night or somebody shot him. It looked like suicide. Perhaps you'd like to examine that desk you were just looking at and see if your gun's there."

Lyster crossed the room with quick strides. He opened the drawer. He said: "Good heavens—the pistol's gone."

Callaghan raised his eyebrows. He said: "So the pistol's gone. And you went for a walk last night to St. John's Wood to see Raven. But you didn't go into the house. Well, I hope the police believe your story, Lyster."

Lyster said: "But they must believe it. They . . ."

Callaghan said: "Take it easy." He held out his cigarette case in a gloved hand towards Lyster. He said: "Have a cigarette and relax. If you didn't do it, you'll be all right."

Lyster took the case, opened it, took a cigarette, lit it. His fingers were trembling. He handed the case back.

Callaghan said: "Well, I'll be on my way."

*

Back in the office he handed the cigarette case to Nikolls. He said: "Check the prints on that case, Windy. They're Lyster's."

Nikolls answered: "If they're the same as the one's I took off the butt of that gun he's the guy."

Callaghan grinned at him. "That's right, Windy," he said. "Now get going."

Outside the evening rain beat on the window pane. Callaghan sat relaxed in his office chair, a cigarette hanging from one corner of his mouth. He was playing a tattoo on his blotting pad with his fingers.

Effie Thompson came in. She said: "Mr. Callaghan, Mrs. Raven is here."

Callaghan said: "Show her in." He got to his feet as the woman came into the office. She wore a black coat and skirt underneath her fur coat, and a small, very smart, tailor-made hat.

Callaghan said: "I think you look wonderful. Won't you sit down?"

She sat down in the chair opposite his desk. He went on: "I'm sorry about your husband, Mrs. Raven."

She looked at him. She said: "Are you surprised? I told you he intended to commit suicide."

Callaghan nodded. He lit a cigarette. He said: "Yes. That's too bad. That means to say you don't get the five thousand pounds from your uncle."

She shook her head. She said: "No." She smiled at him. "I've been lucky. I saw him this morning. And he realizes what an outsider my husband was. He's given me the money. I'm glad because now I can pay you a proper fee, Mr. Callaghan."

Callaghan said: "That's marvellous." There was a pause, then he went on: "You know, Mrs. Raven, your husband didn't commit suicide."

She looked at him in astonishment. "No?"

"No," repeated Callaghan. "I went round to the St. John's Wood house after our first interview. I found him lying by the side of the armchair in front of the fire. I must say it looked like suicide."

She said: "It was suicide, surely."

Callaghan raised his eyebrows. "You really think so?" he said. He went on: "I got my assistant Nikolls round and we took the fingerprints off the gun. They were the prints of your boy friend Mr. Lyster. If it had been suicide they should have been the prints of your husband. They weren't. And Lyster had no alibi. He told me that he went round that evening to see your husband to have a showdown with him, that he changed his mind and went away. Incidentally, the gun belonged to Lyster."

She said: "My God! So Eustace killed him."

Callaghan said casually: "Yes, that's what the police would have thought, but I didn't see why they should. I didn't think it was a good idea. You see, Mrs. Raven, you're my client and I knew you were in love with Lyster. I knew you wouldn't want him pulled in on a murder charge."

She looked at him steadily. She said: "So . . .?"

Callaghan said: "So I cleaned the prints off the butt of the gun."

She said: "Wasn't that an extraordinary thing to do. Surely there ought to have been some prints on the gun. Somebody must have held it."

Callaghan said: "No, the prints of the person who shot your husband never appeared on it."

She moved a little in her chair. She said: "Exactly what do you mean?"

Callaghan said: "I mean you killed Raven." He looked at her. He was smiling.

She said: "Mr. Callaghan, I think you must be mad."

"No," said Callaghan. "I'm not mad—merely intelligent. You see, I had an idea that I'd like to keep an eye on you, so when I left the house after I'd found your husband's body, and we'd taken the prints off the gun, I got Nikolls to keep an eye on you. He's been on your tail for the last two days. He knows about the gentleman you've been meeting—the man you're really in love with."

She looked at Callaghan. Her eyes were like burning coals.

He said: "You killed Raven before you even came to see me. Quite a clever idea, you know."

She laughed—a brittle laugh. She said: "Really, Mr. Callaghan, having regard to the fact that my husband telephoned you and warned you against me just before I came into your office, it would be difficult to know how I could have killed him."

Callaghan said: "Nevertheless, you killed him. You see, he didn't telephone me. The man who telephoned me was the man you've been visiting during the last two days—not Lyster. Lyster was just your stooge." He went on: "About seven o'clock on the night that you came to see me, you had a talk with your husband in the sitting-room at St. John's Wood. You had stolen the automatic pistol from Lyster's desk, but you never handled it with your hands. You were wearing gloves. You carried it inside that muff that you had on the night you came to see me.

"Well . . . you went up near to your husband. You put the muff close to his head, and you shot him. You held the gun so close that there'd be powder marks round the wound. Then you put the gun by his side. The only fingerprints on it were Lyster's. You knew that. I rather think you encouraged Lyster to go and have an interview with your husband that night. He was stupid enough to go, but he didn't see your husband because he couldn't get in. He rang the doorbell but nobody answered. Then you came to see me. You knew I wasn't in my office. You'd watched me leave. You came afterwards. You sent my assistant out to find me. You'd probably seen me go into the bar round the corner. You waited outside in the darkness. When you saw me come back to the office you telephoned your boy friend No. 2, and he rang through pretending to be your husband. He warned me against you—a very clever scheme."

He yawned. "That's why you made the fire up and turned on the electric fire in the St. John's Wood sitting-room before you left, so that the body should still be warm, so that *rigor mortis* wouldn't set in, so that the police doctor couldn't say within an hour or two as to what time Raven was actually killed."

He looked at her. She said nothing. Callaghan went on: "A marvellous idea. You got rid of Raven. Lyster would have been picked up for the murder if the police had seen his prints on the gun, if they'd known he'd been round to the St. John's Wood house on that night. And you'd have got your five thousand pounds and the man you want. As it is . . ." He shrugged his shoulders.

There was a knock at the door. Effie Thompson came in. She said: "Mr. Callaghan, the police car's here. Detective-Inspector Gringall is waiting outside."

Callaghan got up. He said: "Well, they've come for you, Mrs. Raven."

She said in a hard voice: "You're damned clever, Callaghan. But it was a good scheme."

Callaghan said: "Not too bad. Somebody once said that the criminal always makes a silly mistake. You made it."

She smiled. She looked very beautiful. She said: "Tell me my mistake, Mr. Callaghan."

Callaghan said: "At your first interview I asked you how your husband knew you were coming to see me. You told me you'd left the telephone book open, that you'd scored underneath my name, with your fingernail, that he would realize you'd been me." He stubbed out his cigarette on the ashtray.

She said: "Well . . .?"

Callaghan said: "Well, you see, Mrs. Raven, my telephone number isn't in the telephone book."

6
IN THE HALL

IT WAS beginning to get dark. Callaghan got up, pulled the black-out curtains. He went back to his desk, opened a drawer, took out a quart bottle of Bourbon whisky and a glass. He poured out four fingers, handed it to the man who sat slumped in the chair opposite the desk. He said: "Drink this, Lennan. And stop jittering. Tell me exactly what happened."

Lennan drank some of the whisky, took the cigarette offered him. He said: "Frayle wanted to see me to-night. He said he'd got to see me to-night. I know exactly what he wanted to see me about. He had me in a corner. I owed him four thousand pounds. He'd got something on me. He wanted the four thousand I'd taken him for. But he didn't mind losing the money so much—it was the fact that I'd been a bit too clever for him that annoyed him. He wanted to know how I'd done it."

Callaghan said: "So he'd got something on you, had he?"

Lennan nodded.

"All right," said Callaghan. "Go on."

Lennan gulped down the rest of the whisky. He said: "I thought there'd be a hell of a row, so I suggested he'd better come round to my flat. I arranged that with him on the telephone. I told him if he'd be at the flat just before seven to-night, I'd get there as soon as I could. I told him I wasn't quite certain as to what time I could get there, that I was going to spend the day trying to think out some way of getting some money for him. I sent him round the door key in an envelope with a note. I told him to let himself into the flat and wait for me."

Callaghan asked: "Any other keys to the flat?"

Lennan shook his head. "No," he said. "That key was the only key in existence. I was worried sick," he went on. "I knew I'd got to think out something—some way out of the jam. This afternoon I took a train out to the golf course. I've always found it easier to think on a golf course. Well, I couldn't think. I came back to London. I told you I wasn't looking forward to my interview with Frayle."

Callaghan asked: "What time did you get back?"

"A few minutes before seven," said Lennan. "I went into the Clover Leaf Club. That's about three minutes' walk from my flat. I felt I needed a little Dutch courage. I went into the bar and had three double whiskies and sodas."

"And then you went round to the flat?" Callaghan asked.

Lennan said: "No, I didn't. I went out of the bar and took my golf clubs upstairs. I put them in the cloakroom. There was nobody looking after it. I hung about the cloakroom and walked up and down the passage outside." He grinned feebly. "Between you and me and the doorpost," he went on, "I was scared of the meeting with Frayle. I knew he was going to be damned tough. Eventually, quite a time afterwards—it must have been somewhere round about a quarter to eight—I went downstairs and began to walk towards the flat. The devil of it is nobody saw me go out. Nobody knew I was hanging about upstairs all that time."

Callaghan said: "I see. The girl in the bar on the first floor is going to say you were only there a few minutes?"

Lennan ran his tongue over his lips. "That's right," he said. "When I got to the apartment block I walked upstairs to my flat on the first floor and rang the bell. There was no answer. I stood there for about five minutes. Then I thought that possibly Frayle had got fed up and gone away. But I knew he wouldn't do that. I knew he'd be there. I wondered what was the matter. Then I got an idea. At the end of the passage outside is a chair. I went and got it, stood on it and looked through the ventilator that's about three feet over the top of the doorway—just a little slit.

"I looked through into the hallway of the flat and I saw Frayle lying there half way between the door and the telephone table on the far side of the hall. I could see he was dead all right."

"I see," said Callaghan. "And what did you do then?"

"I lost my head," said Lennan. "I got off the chair, put it back, went out and started walking about the streets. I realized I was in a bad jam."

Callaghan asked: "Why? Why were you in a bad jam?"

Lennan said: "Listen. Everybody knows that I hate Frayle like hell, I've said half a dozen times I'd like to kill him. All right. It's known that he had an appointment with me at seven o'clock. The girl in the Clover Leaf Club is going to say that I left there at three or four minutes past seven. She's not going to know I was hanging about there until nearly a quarter to eight upstairs. I can't account for that half hour, see? Everybody's going to believe that I was waiting for Frayle and shot him."

Callaghan said: "Who's going to believe that? Who knows you had an appointment with him?"

"His partner, Varney, for one," said Lennan. "Varney's not a bad chap. Varney doesn't dislike me. He tried to put the brake on Frayle over this business, but Frayle wouldn't listen. Varney knew about that meeting."

Callaghan said: "If Varney didn't dislike you, and he was Frayle's partner, why couldn't he influence Frayle to be a little more reasonable about you?"

Lennan grinned cynically. "You don't know Frayle," he said. "Varney's his partner all right, but only in a small way. He has to do what Frayle tells him. Everybody has to do what Frayle wants. You don't know Frayle."

Callaghan said: "No. It looks as if I never shall now, doesn't it?"

Lennan said: "Well, I walked about the streets for half an hour. Then I knew I'd got to do something about it. I'd heard about you from a man I did some business with. You handled an insurance case for him. I thought I'd come round and see you."

Callaghan said: "And what am I supposed to do?"

Lennan said: "I don't know. Can't you do anything?"

Callaghan grinned. He said: "Yes. There's one thing we can do right anyway. We'll tell the police about this."

He took up the telephone.

Callaghan finished his whisky and soda, lit a cigarette. He said to the girl behind the Clover Leaf Club bar: "Do you remember Mr. Lennan coming in here last night?"

She said: "Oh yes. He was here for a few minutes. I remember noticing he drank three double whiskies and sodas in five minutes. I thought he looked ill."

Callaghan asked: "Do you know what he did when he left the bar?"

She said: "No. All I know is he went out. He took his golf clubs with him. I thought he was going." She went on: "There was a murder in his flat, wasn't there? I read about it in the mid-day paper. I'm sorry for Mr. Lennan."

Callaghan said: "Yes. So am I. So long!"

He went out of the bar. He closed the door quietly behind him. He stood for a moment on the landing, then he turned and walked up the stairs. On the second floor was a room used as a writing room and library. It was empty. Callaghan went up to the third floor. On the right of the landing was a cloakroom, on the left was a passage-way, with windows on the far side.

Callaghan went into the cloakroom. In the far corner, leaning up against a telephone call box, he saw a golf bag, covered and locked. From where he stood he could recognize Lennan's initials. He threw away his cigarette stub, lit a fresh one. He walked out of the cloakroom across the landing and along the passage. One of the windows was open. Callaghan leaned on the window-sill and looked out. His mind was so concentrated on the Frayle killing that it was quite three or four minutes before he realized that he was looking, across an open space, at the back windows of the apartment house in which Lennan lived. Opposite him, two floors down, a window was open. Callaghan calculated that the window was only fifty yards away at most.

He drew back from the window, stood in the passage smoking quietly. After a few minutes he went back to the cloakroom. He crossed over to where Lennan's golf bag was. He took a key ring out of his pocket and began operations. Two minutes afterwards the bag was unlocked. Callaghan whistled quietly. In the bag, with a golf club over the butt, was a medium calibre sporting rifle.

Callaghan put the cover on the bag, locked the padlock. He threw his cigarette away and went out.

Chief Detective-Inspector Gringall said: "I'm glad you came along, Slim. It makes things easier. This is a new idea for murder suspects to go running round to private detectives, isn't it? What did he think you could do?"

Callaghan said: "I don't know. But I don't like it. It smells."

Gringall nodded. He said: "Lennan got back to London some time before seven. He went to the Clover Leaf Club. He spent a few minutes in the bar. Then he went upstairs in the cloakroom."

Callaghan raised his eyebrows. "How did you know?" he asked.

"His golf bag was there," said Gringall. "There was no one on duty in the cloakroom—the attendant's been called up—so Lennan must have taken it up himself. The point is," said Gringall, "just how long was he up there?"

Callaghan asked: "What does the medical evidence say?"

"Frayle was shot about seven o'clock," said Gringall. "Just about seven o'clock. They were able to get pretty near the exact time." He leaned back in his chair, began to fill his pipe. "I wonder why Frayle was in the hall," he said. "There's no doubt about it that he had the only key. There's only one key to that flat and it was found in

Frayle's pocket in an envelope with a note from Lennan confirming what he told you about having sent the key round to Frayle."

Callaghan said: "What do you think?"

Gringall shrugged his shoulders. "The obvious thing to think would be that Frayle was on his way to open the door for someone when he was shot."

Callaghan lit a cigarette. He said casually: "Did any of your people look in Lennan's golf bag by any chance?"

Gringall nodded. "You mean the rifle? Yes, we found that. It had been fired recently. Lennan could have shot Frayle quite easily from the third floor back of the Clover Leaf Club, from the window in the passageway leading from the cloakroom. It faced on to the back of the apartment block where Lennan has his flat, and the window at the rear of the hall of the flat was open."

Callaghan asked: "What about the bullet? Can you check it with the rifle?"

Gringall said: "No. Somebody had been very clever. The bullet that killed Frayle could have been fired from that rifle, but whoever fired that shot knew a thing or two. The nose had been cut off the bullet and there must have been several cuts across the face of it. So that when it hit Frayle it spread like a penny."

Callaghan said: "He must have been reading detective stories." He got up. "Well, I'm glad I've talked to you, Gringall," he said. "I wasn't a bit happy-"

Gringall said: "That's all right. You haven't broken faith with your client." He sighed. "The thing I don't like about this case is that it looks so bad for Lennan. It almost looks as if he's been trying to frame himself for the murder, doesn't it?"

Callaghan said: "I know. That's the way I thought—"

Gringall interrupted: "What did *you* think?"

Callaghan stopped at the doorway. He said: "It looks like a red herring to me. I had an idea that Lennan had planted all this just because he'd killed Frayle some other way. See?"

"I see," said Gringall.

Varney was sitting in the waiting-room when Callaghan got back to the office. He said: "I'm John Varney—Frayle's partner. Lennan rang me up and said he'd been to see you. I felt it was my duty to come round and see you about it."

Callaghan said: "Come into my office, Mr. Varney. So you know something about this?"

Varney said: "I know plenty about it. Normally I should have gone down to Scotland Yard, but as Lennan came to you, and you're sort of representing him, I thought I'd come here first. Then you could do what you liked."

Callaghan sat down at his desk. He said: "Righto! Sit down, have a cigarette and go ahead."

Varney took a cigarette from the silver box and lit it. Callaghan thought he was a well set-up man, that his expression was frank and open. He looked good.

Varney said: "Lennan didn't kill Frayle. I can prove it, and I'm quite prepared to go into the box and do so."

Callaghan said: "That's interesting."

Varney went on: "I knew what the situation was. I knew about the trouble between Lennan and Frayle.

Strangely enough, in an odd sort of way I sympathized with both of them."

Callaghan said: "How do you know that Lennan didn't kill Frayle?"

"I'll tell you," said Varney. "Frayle told me that he was going round to see Lennan, that he was going to wait for him at his flat. He was rather enjoying the situation. He knew that Lennan was half mad with worry, that he was going to spend the day trying to raise that four thousand pounds. Frayle rather liked the idea of sitting there like a spider waiting for the fly to come into the web. Because even if Lennan had raised the four thousand—which was more or less an impossibility—Frayle was still going to make it hot for him. You see, Lennan had twisted Frayle for that four thousand. Frayle's idea was to get the whole story from Lennan as to how he'd done it, get what money Lennan could raise—if he could raise any—and then turn him over to the police at the end of it."

"I see," said Callaghan. "Not a very nice fellow, this Frayle?"

"Not very," said Varney. "I've been his partner for five years. He was a good business man but a nasty person to work with. I don't know how I stuck it."

Callaghan said: "All right. So much for Frayle. Now tell me about Lennan."

Varney said: "I was curious about one or two things. I knew that Frayle was going round to Lennan's place fairly early. I wondered whether he was going to take a police officer with him. The other thing I wondered about was whether Lennan would turn up. My own idea was that that boyo was going to make a getaway while the going was good. So I thought I'd satisfy my curiosity on both points."

He drew on his cigarette, inhaled, blew the smoke out slowly. "Just opposite the apartment house where Lennan lives," he said, "a little further down the street, is a tobacconist. I knew the girl in the shop. I planted myself there just before seven o'clock. I watched the entrance of the apartment house. At a couple of minutes to seven—that was the exact time because there's a clock on the wall of the tobacconist's shop—I saw Frayle go in. He was taking the envelope which I suppose contained Lennan's key out of his breast pocket as he went in. I watched. I wanted to see if Lennan was going to turn up. Well, he didn't. I waited till about five and twenty minutes to eight. Then I got fed up. I lit a cigarette and had made up my mind to go off home. Just as I was leaving the shop I saw Lennan come round the corner. He was walking slowly and he certainly looked as if he wasn't looking forward to the interview. I watched him go into the apartment block. Then I went off home."

Callaghan said: "That puts Lennan in the clear. The police doctor's been lucky in this case. He's been able to determine practically exactly the time of death. It was just about seven. So if Lennan didn't turn up till twenty minutes to eight that lets him out."

"That's what I thought," said Varney.

Callaghan said: "The interesting point now is how the murderer whoever he was—got into the flat."

Varney nodded. "Somebody must have got in," he said. "And there were a lot of people who didn't like Frayle."

Callaghan nodded. "A man with many enemies," he said.

Varney got up. "If you want me, or if you want me to tell my story to the police, let me know," he said.

Callaghan said: "I will."

Varney went out.

For an hour after Varney had gone, Callaghan sat, his feet on the desk, blowing smoke rings. He yawned, threw his cigarette stub into the fireplace, took his feet off the desk, reached for the telephone.

When Gringall came on the line, Callaghan said: "About this Frayle thing, I've got an idea."

"You don't say?" said Gringall. "That's strange, isn't it?"

Callaghan said: "Believe it or not, but I have. Listen: there's no other suspect outside Lennan, is there?"

Gringall said: "No! And I don't even know that Lennan is a suspect. I don't think we've got anything on which we can charge Lennan. Incidentally, he was using that rifle to shoot rabbits on the golf course. That's a habit of his. That accounts for it being used. What's in your head, Slim?"

Callaghan said: "This murder is a co-operative business between Lennan and Varney. It's a nice job. It's so good I doubt whether you'll ever prove it."

Gringall said: "Really! Go on."

Callaghan said: "Lennan took Frayle for four thousand pounds. Frayle was more interested in finding out just how Lennan had done that than he was getting the money back. But he was going to get back what money he could from Lennan, promise him immunity, and when he got the story out of him, turn him over to the police. Lennan didn't know that, but Varney did. Frayle told him, and Varney wasn't going to have that, because he was the man who helped Lennan take Frayle for the four thousand. So they make a little arrangement.

"Everybody is going to suspect Lennan, so they build up a nice case against him. First of all he has a rifle. Secondly, he goes upstairs to the third floor of the Clover Leaf Club which looks out on the hall window of the flat. Thirdly, if it had come to a show-down we'd have found that Lennan only had a few rounds of ammunition when he went on the golf course, and that he used every one of them there. That would have got him out.

"The next thing," Callaghan went on, "is the key. Nobody has got a key to that flat except Frayle, who's inside the flat when he's killed. So he must have been shot from the outside. He was shot from outside. He was shot through the ventilator above the doorway, but in order to do this, Frayle had to be in the hall of the flat. He had to be immediately in line with that ventilator."

Gringall said: "Very interesting. Go on, Slim."

"It's easy," said Callaghan. "Both Varney and Lennan know that there's no attendant in the cloakroom at the Clover Leaf Club, and there's no hall porter in Lennan's apartment block. You got that?"

"I got it," said Gringall.

"At ten minutes to seven," Callaghan went on, "Varney went into Lennan's apartment block, went up to the first floor and hid round the bend in the corridor. He knew that Frayle would be arriving there a few minutes before seven. Frayle arrived and went into the flat. He left his things in the hall, went across and sat down in the drawing-room beyond. While he's doing this Varney places the chair, which Lennan has conveniently left around the turn in the corridor, in front of the flat door.

"At this time Lennan finishes his drink at the Clover Leaf Club, goes upstairs to the cloakroom and rings up his own flat on the telephone from the call box. Frayle comes out to answer the telephone in the hall. Lennan pretends he's got a wrong number. Frayle replaces the receiver and turns away. Then Varney shoots him through the ventilator. He can't miss him. Varney replaces the chair, leaves the apartment block, walks quickly over to the tobacconist's shop where he informs the girl he is going to wait to see if Lennan turns up, the idea being that he has arrived there straight from his house.

"He waits there until twenty minutes to eight in order to alibi Lennan. How do you like that?"

Gringall said: "I like it a lot. I like it so much I'm going to pinch those two birds."

Callaghan said: "Listen, it looks as if I'm getting my own client arrested. Who's going to pay my expenses in this case?"

Gringall said: "I wouldn't know. If you're lucky, I'll buy you a drink. So long, Slim."

7
THE BIG BLUFF

WHEN Nikolls came in, Callaghan was slumped back in the big leather chair. His feet were on the desk. He was smoking a cigarette, blowing smoke rings, watching them sail across the office. He said: "Well?"

Nikolls said: "She's outside. She's a looker, this baby. She's got something. But she ain't so happy. Are you gonna see her?"

Callaghan said: "Yes, why not? Ask her to come in." He added as an afterthought: "You wouldn't be happy if you were a good-looking woman and your *fiancé* had just been murdered."

Nikolls said: "No. But I ain't a good-lookin' woman." He grinned. "If I was I wouldn't be workin' here." He went out of the office.

A minute later the girl came in. She was tall, slim, raven-haired, attractive. A great deal of allure, Callaghan thought. Her eyes were red with weeping.

Callaghan got up. He said: "Good morning, Miss Allardyce. I'm sorry about all this business, but I don't see how I can be very much use to you. After all, this is really a matter for the police, isn't it? Won't you sit down?" He pushed a chair forward. "Smoke a cigarette and relax," he said.

He gave her a cigarette, lit it, went back to the fireplace. He stood in front of it, his hands behind his back, looking at her. He said: "The story as I know it, Miss Allardyce, is this: Two days ago Eustace Giles, the man to whom you were engaged to be married, threw himself out of a window into the back courtyard of the Aylesbury Arms—an apartment block near St. John's Wood. That is what the police thought first of all, but the post mortem produced a rather interesting theory. The police surgeon discovered that Giles hadn't committed suicide, that he'd been murdered. Somebody had hit him over the head with a heavy instrument of some sort and then pushed him out of the window in the hope that it would appear to be suicide. Am I right?"

She nodded. She said: "That's perfectly right, Mr. Callaghan."

He said: "Well, what can I do about that? The police believe that somebody killed him and I expect they'll find the murderer. They do, you know, very often—more often than people believe, and they'll probably do it much more successfully than I should."

She said miserably: "That's the whole point, Mr. Callaghan. The police think they have found the murderer, and they're wrong."

Callaghan raised his eyebrows. He said: "Really?"

She said: "I ought to tell you the story from the beginning. You see, I was in love or thought I was in love with another man before I met Eustace. A very charming and delightful man—rather older than myself, it's true—but still a man of great character. We'd been friends for quite a time. He thought that we were going to be married. He'd planned for it." She shrugged her shoulders unhappily. "Then," she went on, "I met Eustace."

Callaghan asked: "What is this other man's name?"

"Edward Strangeways," she said. "He's the person I'm worried about."

Callaghan threw his cigarette stub in the fireplace, lit a fresh one. He said: "Why are you worried about Strangeways?"

She said: "The police believe he killed Eustace. You see, they've made enquiries—exhaustive enquiries. They think he was the last person to see Eustace."

Callaghan said: "I see." He inhaled tobacco smoke. He asked: "Have the police done anything about it yet?"

She said: "No, but I know that Edward's solicitors believe that they're going to arrest him."

Callaghan smiled at her. He said: "You know, Miss Allardyce, the police, in this country at any rate, do not consider arresting a man merely because he was the last person to see the man who was believed to have been murdered. They must have other evidence. They must believe there was a motive."

She said: "That's the trouble, Mr. Callaghan. There was a motive."

Callaghan cocked one eyebrow. He said: "Really? Do you know what it was?"

She nodded. She said: "You see, Eustace wasn't what is usually called a good man. In point of fact I believe he was a very bad man. His life had been one long series of affairs with women. Lots of people disliked him." She went on: "Don't misunderstand me, Mr. Callaghan. I know he'd given up all that sort of thing. After he'd met me he'd turned over a new leaf. He never made any secret of his life. He told me all about himself. I believed him and I loved him."

Callaghan said: "I understand. And I suppose that the other man—Strangeways—also knew about Eustace and his rather lurid past?"

She said: "Yes. In fact I told him about it. Right from the first he was quite naturally against me having anything to do with Eustace. I understood that. Men are just as jealous as women are. He entreated me not to have anything to do with Eustace—not to go on with this idea of marrying him. I told him he was stupid. I told him how Eustace had done every possible thing he could to prove he was serious about me."

"Every possible thing?" said Callaghan. "Now what would that mean, Miss Allardyce? You see, I'm trying to get all the facts."

She said: "Well, one of the things about Eustace was his extravagance with women. He had an income and Edward thought that once we were married he'd go back to his old sort of life, throwing himself and his money away on odd women. I told him that wasn't so. I told him that Eustace had actually made a settlement on me already, to prove to me that he was serious about us."

Callaghan said: "Well, didn't that put Strangeways more at ease?"

She nodded. "It did at first," she said, "but apparently a few days ago he heard something about Eustace—something about some other woman. I don't know what it was. Apparently he made up his mind to go round and see Eustace. I ought to have known—"

Callaghan interrupted quickly: "Why ought you to have known?"

She said: "Edward rang me up and asked me to give him Eustace's address. I did so. After I'd hung up the receiver I wondered why he wanted it. My instinct should have warned me. I ought to have known there was going to be trouble. I ought never to have given him the address."

"But," said Callaghan, "you did give him the address. And he went round and saw Eustace. Is that right? On the day that his body was found."

She nodded. When Callaghan looked at her he saw that her eyes were full of tears. She said: "Yes. I believe from what I can hear from his solicitors that he went round there in the late afternoon. Eustace's body was found that evening. Apparently nobody saw him after Edward."

Callaghan said: "It doesn't look as if there's an awful lot wrong with the police theory, does it?"

She said: "Everything's wrong with it."

Callaghan said: "If you believe that, it means you have an alternative theory, Miss Allardyce. If you believe that Strangeways didn't kill Giles, then presumably you've got some idea in your head as to who did."

She leaned forward in her chair. She said: "Mr. Callaghan, I've told you about Eustace and women. There were a lot of women who disliked him intensely. The news of our engagement and impending marriage had just become public. Don't you see what I mean?"

Callaghan nodded. He said: "Yes, I see what you mean. You mean that one of Eustace's lady friends had heard that he intended to turn over a new leaf and didn't like it. That they went round to see him and killed him, threw his body out of the window. Is that right?"

She said: "Yes."

Callaghan went on: "That's all very well, but what about the police evidence that nobody saw Giles after Strangeways?"

She said: "There might be an explanation for that. Normally, anybody wanting to go up to Eustace's flat would naturally see the hall-porter. They would have to pass the hall-porter's lodge to reach the lift. But supposing that somebody had a key to the flat. They could go in the back entrance, walk up the stairs. Nobody would see them."

Callaghan said: "I see." He blew another smoke ring. He said: "Had you any reason to believe that Giles feared Strangeways? Had you talked to him about it?"

She said: "Of course I told Eustace all about him—what a fine man he was. We talked about it the last time I saw Eustace alive. That would be a week ago."

Callaghan asked: "What was his reaction to that?"

She said: "There just wasn't any reaction. He said he felt rather sorry for him."

Callaghan said: "Well, Miss Allardyce, what do you want me to do?"

She said: "I'll tell you, Mr. Callaghan. There's a woman—a woman called Vanessa Jerome. Eustace told me about her. She's been in love with him for a long time. She'd told him that if he ever looked at another woman she'd kill him. I know she had a key to his flat."

Callaghan said: "I see. And you think that she killed him?"

She said: "I feel certain of it. I'll tell you why. I told you just now that Edward Strangeways had heard something about Eustace and another woman—something which made him go round to see Eustace. He'd probably heard that Eustace had started another affair with somebody just at the time when he'd become engaged to me. I believe that this woman Vanessa Jerome was his informant."

Callaghan said: "I've got it. You mean she telephoned and told Strangeways, knowing that he'd go round to see Giles, waited for him to leave, slipped in the back-way and killed Giles?"

She said: "Something like that, Mr. Callaghan. I'm certain this woman killed Eustace. I feel that unless you can do something to help it may be very, very bad for Edward. I'm afraid for him."

Callaghan said: "All right, Miss Allardyce. You go home. Don't worry, just relax. We'll do what we can."

It was three o'clock when Callaghan was shown into Chief Detective-Inspector Gringall's room at Scotland Yard.

Gringall said: "Hello, Slim. I'm glad to see you. What's the trouble?"

Callaghan said: "It's about this Giles murder. Miss Allardyce—the woman who was going to marry him—has been to see me. She's got an idea that you're after the wrong man. She's got an idea that you're going to arrest this fellow Strangeways. She doesn't like it a bit. She's certain that Strangeways would never have killed Giles in a million years. She thinks one of his previous lady friends did it."

Gringall said: "Is that so? I don't agree. She believes Strangeways killed Giles." He looked at Callaghan and smiled. "Possibly she hasn't told you the whole truth," he said. "Sometimes they don't, you know."

Callaghan said: "All right. So she didn't tell me the whole truth. You tell me—why does she think that Strangeways killed Giles—as you're so certain on that point?"

Gringall said: "Giles was killed on the afternoon of the day before yesterday—Tuesday afternoon. Apparently, on the day before that—on the Monday—Strangeways got into touch with Miss Allardyce and asked her for Giles' address. She says she gave it to him, and then was sorry afterwards."

Callaghan nodded. He said. "That's right. That's what she told me."

"And there's something else that apparently she didn't tell you," said Gringall. "She immediately sat down and wrote Giles a letter. She didn't like the idea of this interview between these two men at all. In her letter she told Giles that Strangeways was coming to see him the next day. She asked Giles not to see him. She said there would only be trouble, that Strangeways was in a hell of a temper and hated the very mention of Giles' name."

Callaghan said: "That's not so good. You found the letter?"

"That's right," said Gringall. "We found it in pieces in the wastepaper basket in Giles' flat. I had 'em pasted together. Perhaps you'd like to read it."

He laid the pasted up letter and envelope on the desk in front of Callaghan. He said: "It looks pretty bad for Strangeways, doesn't it? He was the last person to see Giles alive. I'm sorry about your client, Slim, but I think to-morrow we'll probably have to pull him in."

Callaghan said: "Well I can't stop you." He glanced at the pasted up envelope in front of him. He said: "I've got Giles' address from this envelope I suppose you've no objection to my going and looking round the flat?"

Gringall said: "Certainly not. There's no reason why you shouldn't. I'll call through the porter downstairs and tell him it's O.K."

Callaghan said: "Don't do that—if you don't mind, Gringall. I want to try something."

Gringall shrugged his shoulders. "Just as you like, Slim," he said.

Callaghan slipped quietly into the back entrance of the Aylesbury Arms. He met nobody. He walked up to the second floor, along the long corridor, till he came to No. 12—Giles' flat. He realized that his client was speaking the truth when she said someone could get to the flat quite easily without passing the hall-porter.

Callaghan tried the door of the flat. It was locked. He was just moving away when the sound of footsteps came along the corridor. A postman appeared. Callaghan said: "Listen, postman. You deliver the letters here? Do you remember delivering a letter that would probably arrive by the afternoon post to this flat—a letter for Mr. Giles—two days ago?"

The postman said: "I might have delivered a letter to Mr. Giles, but not to that flat. He lived on the floor above."

Callaghan said: "Thank you very much." He went downstairs, walked round the block, went in the front entrance. He stopped at the hall-porter's box. He said: "Perhaps you wouldn't mind answering a question or two? Mr. Giles—the man who was killed here two days ago—lived on the third floor. When did he move to the second floor?"

"The afternoon he was killed," said the hall-porter. "He only went down there for a few hours. You see he was leaving—going abroad—the next day."

Callaghan said: "I see. Why did he move out of his own flat?"

"One of the water pipes burst," said the porter. "The place was almost flooded."

Callaghan said: "Thank you very much." He gave the man a ten shilling note, walked out of the building. Fifty yards down the road, Callaghan found a telephone call box. He went inside, rang Nikolls, gave him some instructions. Then he came out of the telephone box, began to walk in the direction of his office. He was thinking, his hands stuck deep into overcoat pockets.

Arrived, he went straight into his own room. He found Nikolls and Miss Allardyce there. Callaghan took off his hat and overcoat.

She said: "I came directly Mr. Nikolls telephoned me. You've discovered something, Mr. Callaghan?"

Callaghan said: "Yes. I've discovered that Strangeways didn't kill Giles."

She smiled. "I'm so glad," she said. "So my theory about the other woman was right?"

"No," said Callaghan. "It wasn't a bit right. There was only one person who could have killed Giles. You killed him."

She gazed at him with wide-open eyes. She said: "You must be mad, Mr. Callaghan!"

Callaghan shrugged his shoulders. He said coolly: "You didn't tell me that on Monday last, the day before Giles was murdered, when Strangeways asked you for Giles' address, so that he could go and see him, you wrote a letter to Giles entreating him not to see Strangeways, saying that only bad could come of the interview. You didn't tell me that, did you?"

She shook her head. "No," she said, "I didn't. I thought that might make it look worse for Edward."

Callaghan said: "Rubbish. You know, Miss Allardyce, the criminal—even the most clever one—always makes a mistake. You did. You made a very bad mistake. The letter you wrote to Giles on Monday last, and posted that evening, the day before he was killed, was addressed to No. 12 Aylesbury Arms. I got the address from the envelope."

She looked at him. "I don't know what you mean," she said.

Callaghan went on: "Giles lived on the floor above No. 12. He only moved downstairs on the afternoon he was murdered. He moved because a water pipe burst in his own flat. He didn't even know himself that he was going to move until the pipe burst. So how did you know the day before?"

She said nothing. Nikolls looked at her sideways—watching her.

Callaghan went on: "But that letter was posted and there was a perfectly good Monday evening postmark on it. Well . . . there's only one explanation for that . . .?"

She said dully: "Perhaps you can explain that too!"

Callaghan said: "Quite easily. You knew that Strangeways was going to see Giles on Tuesday afternoon. So you wrote that letter to him suggesting that he shouldn't see Strangeways, that Strangeways was after his blood. Then you addressed an envelope to yourself in pencil and posted it. You got that in the normal course of post on Tuesday morning. You rubbed out the pencil address, leaving a blank envelope with a cancelled stamp and postmark on it. Right?"

She said: "You're being very interesting, Mr. Callaghan. Please go on."

"You put your letter inside that envelope," said Callaghan, "and you went round to the Aylesbury Arms in the afternoon. You went in the back way and you waited in the second floor passage to see when Strangeways came down from the floor above—from Giles' flat. But he didn't come down from the floor above. He came out of No. 12—on the second floor—and you realized that Giles had moved his flat."

Callaghan lit a cigarette slowly. "You went in. You talked with Giles. He confirmed your suspicions that he was planning to leave the country, that he was going to walk out on you—probably with your rival, Miss Vanessa Jerome. So you hit him over the head and then pushed him out of the window into the back courtyard. Then you planted your letter to him. And not knowing how long he had been in No. 12—not knowing that he'd only been there an hour or so—you wrote that address on the envelope, tore the envelope and letter into little pieces and threw them into the waste-paper basket. You knew the police would piece them together. And you knew that letter would hang Strangeways for the crime you had committed."

She began to laugh. She said: "Very nice circumstantial evidence, Mr. Callaghan. But not very easy to prove."

Callaghan said: "Quite easy. I got the police to check on the envelope and notepaper for fingerprints. On that notepaper should have been the fingerprints of Giles and yourself. The only fingerprints found were yours, and on the envelope yours and the post people's. Giles' fingerprints were on neither the envelope nor the notepaper. There's the answer."

She shrugged her shoulders. She said: "Oh . . . well . . ."

Effie Thompson came in. "The police officers are here, Mr. Callaghan," she said.

Nikolls squirted some soda-water into Callaghan's glass. He said: "That was a dam good bit of reasoning, Slim. But how the hell did you find out the fingerprints in that time?"

Callaghan said: "I didn't. That was the big bluff—and it came off!"

8
THE MISSING BULLET

A HEAVY gust of wind blew the black-out curtains to one side as Nikolls pushed open the entrance doors to the hall of the Staple Inn at Pinmill. The hall-porter said: "Be careful of the black-out, sir."

Nikolls shook the water from the brim of his hat, took his handkerchief from the breast pocket of his overcoat to wipe the rain from his face. "I like that," he said. "You try walkin' against the wind outside, pal. What a night! Say, is this the Staple Inn?"

The hall-porter said: "Yes, sir."

"Is Mr. Callaghan here?" asked Nikolls.

"He arrived about eleven o'clock—half an hour ago, sir. He's in number nine on the first floor. Are you Mr. Nikolls?"

"Yes," said Nikolls. "I'll go up. Don't bother."

Nikolls crossed the lounge to the staircase, went up to the first floor. Callaghan was sitting in an armchair by the electric fire when Nikolls came into the room. He said: "Hello, Windy. You got here pretty quickly."

"You're tellin' me," said Nikolls. "I've been wanderin' about the goddamned countryside tryin' to find this place. I nearly fell in the river about four times. Say, what is all this about?"

Callaghan said: "Read that."

Nikolls took the envelope that Callaghan held out to him, extracted the letter. He read:

Steam Yacht *Paloma*—Off Pinmill.

Dear Mr. Callaghan,

I should be grateful if you could meet me to-morrow night at eleven o'clock at the Staple Inn at Pinmill. Please stop anything else you are doing and get down there. This is a matter of life and death. I have every reason to believe that an attempt will be made on my life and—

Sincerely yours,

Eustace Charleston.

Nikolls looked up at Callaghan. He said: "Say, I reckon this guy was tight when he wrote this letter. He finishes in the middle of a sentence. Look at his handwriting too! Have you seen him?"

"Not a sign of him," said Callaghan. "I made some enquiries about this Charleston, and it appears he's an extremely wealthy man—almost a millionaire. His yacht *Paloma* is moored about seventy yards out on the river bend. I think we'll go aboard."

"Listen," said Nikolls, "ain't you treatin' this guy seriously? He was probably cockeyed when he wrote that letter."

Callaghan said: "Never mind, I'm interested. Come on, Windy. Let's go."

He put on a raincoat and his hat, then, followed by Nikolls, went down the stairs and out into the street. They made their way through the darkness down to the river. The wind had dropped but it was still raining.

Nikolls said: "What a helluva night. There's a mist comin' up too. Say, how the hell are we gonna get on this boat?"

"Look along the landing stage and see if you can find a dinghy," said Callaghan. "I'll go the other way. If you find a boat yell out. The Paloma's out there. You can just see her in the mist."

"O.K.," said Nikolls. He walked -a few yards along the landing stage, then he called: "Hey, there's a boat here. It's one of the Paloma's dinghies too, the name's on the stern."

Callaghan appeared at his side. In his hand he held a dilapidated pouch.

"I've found something too," he said.

"Say, what is that?" asked Nikolls.

Callaghan said: "A rubber tobacco pouch. It looks as if it's been in the water. Come on, let's get going." He clambered into the dinghy, followed by Nikolls, who inserted the oars into the rowlocks.

Nikolls said: "Me . . . I always get the tough end of the job. Well, here we go . . ." He started to pull out towards the yacht. "I'm supposed to be a detective," he grumbled, "not a sailor."

Callaghan said: "Well, I hope you're a better detective than you are an oarsman."

As they neared the yacht he shouted: "*Paloma . . .* Ahoy . . .!" There was no answer.

"Maybe there's nobody aboard," said Nikolls.

Callaghan said: "We'll have a look anyway."

The dinghy bumped against the side of the Paloma. Callaghan caught hold of a gangway. He noticed another dinghy tied up to one side. "Tie her up, Windy," he said.

"It's easy to talk like that," said Nikolls. "There's a helluva swell runnin'." He made the rope fast.

They clambered on the gangway and climbed up on board.

"Give them a yell, Windy," said Callaghan. "See if there is anybody aboard."

"Say, is there anybody on this goddam hulk?" shouted Nikolls. There was no reply. Nikolls turned towards Callaghan. "What did I tell you?" he said.

"Let's take a look round," said Callaghan. "Maybe they couldn't hear below."

He began to descend the companionway. Nikolls following behind, grabbed his arm. "Look," he said, "there's a crack of light showin' under the door at the end of the passage."

Callaghan walked along the passage, knocked on the door. As he opened the door he could hear the sound of a woman sobbing.

"Well . . . well . . . well!" said Nikolls.

Seated at a table in the centre of the small saloon was a young and beautiful woman. Her eyes were red with weeping. She looked up. "Who are you?" she asked in a strangled voice.

Callaghan said: "My name is Callaghan. I'm a private detective. And you?"

"I'm Viola Charleston," she said. "Thank God you've come, Mr. Callaghan. I was just trying to summon up sufficient courage to row ashore and get in touch with you."

"What's happened?" asked Callaghan.

"It's quite terrible," she said. "My husband has been shot. He's in the forward cabin. He's dead." She began to sob again.

"Take it easy, Mrs. Charleston," said Callaghan. "Windy, we'll go and have a look."

"O.K.," said Nikolls. "Don't get steamed up, Mrs. Charleston. Have a drink or somethin'. These little things will happen."

Callaghan and Nikolls walked along the passageway till they came to another cabin. Callaghan opened the door, switched on the light.

Nikolls said: "Oh, boy . . . what a mess . . .!"

Stretched out on the floor by a bunk on the far side of the cabin was the body of a man. Callaghan walked across, stood looking down at him. "Not so good, is it?" he said. "Looks as if he's been shot clean through the head at close range."

"Yeah," said Nikolls, "in one side and out the other."

Callaghan said: "See if you can find the bullet. It ought to be in the woodwork on this side of the bunk."

"O.K.," said Nikolls. "Say, this guy wasn't so cockeyed after all when he said he was afraid of his life. Someone was gunnin' for this bozo." He stooped down by the side of the bunk. "Look, here's where the bullet hit, see? Here's the hole, but no bullet. Maybe it fell out, or maybe somebody skewered it out."

Callaghan nodded. He said: "Well, we can't do anything here. I'll get back to Mrs. Charleston. Just have a look round, Windy. See if you can find anything."

Callaghan went back to the saloon. He said: "This is a bad business, Mrs. Charleston. I'm very sorry for you." He paused, then he went on: "This morning I received a letter from your husband telling me he was in fear of his life, asking me to meet him at the Staple Inn at Pinmill. I wondered why he didn't turn up. Now I know the reason."

Mrs. Charleston nodded miserably. "It's awful . . ." she said.

The door opened and Nikolls came in. Callaghan said: "Windy, there's some brandy on the sideboard there. Give Mrs. Charleston a drink."

"O.K.," said Nikolls. "I could do with a snifter myself."

Callaghan lit a cigarette. He stood there silently for a moment thinking. Then he said: "Well, I'm afraid there isn't very much I can do, Mrs. Charleston. This is a job for the police."

Mrs. Charleston put down the glass she held in her hand. She looked alarmed. "No . . . no . . . for God's sake no . . .! Mr. Callaghan, you have got to help me," she said.

Callaghan asked: "Exactly what happened, Mrs. Charleston? Were you here?"

"Yes," she said. "We had a dinner party—my husband, and a friend of mine named Ralph Fergus, and a friend of my husband's—Rupert Duval. We were going to have dinner—the four of us by ourselves—and play cards afterwards. It was to be a sort of celebration."

"Yes?" queried Callaghan. "A celebration of what?"

Mrs. Charleston gulped. "My husband and Ralph Fergus have been quarrelling bitterly over me for months. Ralph has been in love with me for years. He's resented my husband's treatment of me—his meanness. He's threatened him on a dozen occasions. Well, three or four days ago they met in London. As usual they quarreled. Ralph Fergus publicly threatened to kill my husband. When I heard about this I was heartbroken. I'm very fond of Ralph. He's a fine type of man. But I didn't want there to be any bad blood between him and my husband. I rang him up and told him all this business must stop, that they must shake hands and be good friends. I asked him if he would come down here to-night and dine with us and make an end to all this horrible quarrelling and bitterness. He agreed. Then I talked my husband into it. I thought at last there'd be a little peace in my life. I asked Rupert Duval to make the party complete."

"I see," said Callaghan. "Go on, Mrs. Charleston."

"Yesterday afternoon," she continued, "my husband went ashore. For some reason which I don't know he telephoned Ralph. They quarreled over the telephone. When my husband returned he was in a fearful rage. By six o'clock he was quite drunk. He was talking the most utter nonsense, saying that he was certain that Ralph was going to kill him. Then he sat down and wrote that letter to you. He told me he was going to employ you to protect him. You understand?"

"I understand," said Callaghan.

She went on: "I told my husband it was nonsense about Ralph. I knew he couldn't kill anybody. He's much too nice a man. At least I thought that—"

Callaghan interrupted: "But anyway, Mrs. Charleston, Fergus and Duval came down to-day and you had your dinner party?"

She nodded. "They came down in the late afternoon. My husband behaved quite normally. Even then I persuaded myself that all would be well. Oh, Mr. Callaghan, you don't know how hard I worked to try and get them to be friendly. But it soon became obvious even to Mr. Duval—that they disliked each other intensely. About seven o'clock we had cocktails. My husband had allowed the crew to go ashore. We looked after ourselves. As usual, Eustace drank a great deal too much. He was drunk before dinner."

"I see," said Callaghan. "I suppose Fergus did a little drinking too."

"I'm afraid so," said Mrs. Charleston. "It was that sort of atmosphere. Then somebody suggested a shooting match. There's a shooting gallery aft. My husband bet Ralph Fergus that he'd beat him. I thought there was going to be a quarrel then, but Mr. Duval smoothed them down."

Callaghan asked: "Did the shooting match take place, Mrs. Charleston?"

"Yes. We went to the shooting gallery and the three men shot with automatic pistols. My husband has four of them. They're kept in that case over there. They all shot very badly, but the atmosphere cleared a little. Then we dined."

"What happened to the pistols when they'd finished in the shooting gallery, Mrs. Charleston?" asked Callaghan.

"Three of them are back in their case," she said. "One of them is missing."

Callaghan asked: "Who used the missing pistol?"

Mrs. Charleston began to cry. "I don't know," she said. "I don't know."

"Are you sure you don't know?" said Callaghan.

Nikolls said: "It's stickin' outa foot it's the pistol Fergus used. She's tryin' to cover up for him."

"Keep quiet, Windy," said Callaghan. "Go on, Mrs. Charleston. What happened then?"

She tried to pull herself together. Then she went on: "We had dinner. All the time I was praying that nothing would happen. It didn't. Except that my husband drank too much at dinner, and I am afraid that Ralph drank more than is usual. I can understand that. He was angry that he'd ever consented to come down on the yacht. I blame myself for that."

Callaghan asked: "Dinner passed off without any trouble?"

"Yes," she said. "After dinner we began to play poker. My husband's temper got worse and worse. Eventually, after we had been playing for about half an hour, he became positively insulting. I could see that Mr. Duval—he'd been very uncomfortable the whole evening—could stand no more. He said he had an urgent appointment in town, that he must go. He went."

"I see," said Callaghan. "He used one of the two dinghies belonging to the yacht—the one we found tied up to the landing stage?"

"That's right," she said. "He pulled over by himself. I hated him going."

"And then, Mrs. Charleston?" said Callaghan.

She went on: "When I returned after seeing Mr. Duval off we continued to play poker—the three of us. I think that game was the most terrible experience I have ever had in my life. Those two men—my husband and Ralph—

facing each other across the card table with hatred in their eyes."

Callaghan interrupted: "Are you in love with Ralph Fergus, Mrs. Charleston?"

"Yes," she said. "He's been my best friend. He's the soul of honour. There's never been anything between us, Mr. Callaghan. All the years of misery I have spent with my husband—at least, I have had his friendship to rely on. That's why my husband hated him. He didn't want me to have a friend." She began to sob again.

"Go on, Mrs. Charleston," said Callaghan. "What happened next?"

"It got worse and worse," she said. "Eventually, my husband made a particularly rude remark to me. I told him that I would not sit there and be insulted. He laughed. He said that he'd leave me alone with my heart's desire. He got up, staggered out of the saloon. We heard him grope his way towards his cabin."

"And what did you and Mr. Fergus do?" Callaghan asked.

She said: "We sat there. We sat there for quite a little while. Neither of us said anything. Ralph had two or three more drinks. Then suddenly he said: 'By God, I'm not going to stand for this.' He got up and lurched out of the saloon after my husband."

"And you stayed where you were?" asked Callaghan.

"Yes," she answered. "I thought that Ralph was merely going to tell Eustace he was through with him once and for all. I thought he was going to tell him exactly what he thought of him and go. I had no other idea in my mind."

"And then you heard the shot?" said Callaghan.

She nodded. "And then I heard the shot," she repeated. "I was petrified! After a little while Ralph came back. He was laughing. Of course, he was terribly drunk. He didn't know what he'd done. He said: 'Well, you won't be bothered with him anymore.' I forced myself to go along the passageway and look into my husband's cabin. It was terrible. Then I came back. I pleaded with Ralph to get assistance, to send for the police."

Callaghan asked: "What did he do?"

"We took the second dinghy and rowed ashore," she said. "Ralph went off. I sat there in the darkness waiting, but nothing happened. Nobody came. I didn't know what to do."

Callaghan said: "I suppose you thought that Fergus had made a getaway while the going was good?"

"Yes," she said. "And having come to that conclusion I couldn't do anything. I came back here. I've been here ever since trying to make up my mind what I should do."

"There isn't much you can do, is there, Mrs. Charleston? I'm very sorry for you. All we can do is to get in touch with the police. This is a job for them."

Mrs. Charleston said pleadingly: "Mr. Callaghan, you must help Ralph."

"How can I do that?" Callaghan asked. "He hasn't helped himself much by running away."

"He wasn't sober," said Mrs. Charleston. "He wasn't in his right senses. You've got to help me, Mr. Callaghan." Her voice became desperate. "You've got to help us both."

"Well, Mrs. Charleston," said Callaghan. "I came down here to-night to work for your husband. But I don't see why I shouldn't work for you. Maybe we'll find a way out of this. In the meantime, you come ashore with us. You'd better get your coat."

"Very well," she said. She got up, crossed to the door, went out.

Callaghan turned to Nikolls. He said: "Did you find anything of interest in Charleston's cabin?"

"No," said Nikolls. "At least there was one thing that was a bit odd. There was a dressin' gown in a cupboard there. The inside was damp."

"I see," said Callaghan slowly.

Nikolls said: "Why? Whatya thinkin' about?"

"I was wondering what that empty tobacco pouch was doing on the landing stage," said Callaghan.

It was eleven o'clock the next morning when Callaghan walked into his office. His secretary, Effie Thompson, was busy typing.

"Good morning, Effie," said Callaghan. "Have you heard from Mrs. Charleston?"

"Yes, Mr. Callaghan," said Effie. "She's in your office waiting for you."

Callaghan said: "All right, Effie. Let me know when he comes in."

He went into his private office, closed the door behind him. Mrs. Charleston was sitting in the chair by his desk. She looked calm in spite of the tired look in her eyes. She said: "Good morning, Mr. Callaghan. Did you get my message?"

"Yes," said Callaghan. "And Fergus's address. Nikolls is seeing him now."

She said: "Mr. Callaghan, is there nothing we can do? The police—"

Callaghan interrupted: "Don't worry too much, Mrs. Charleston. The first thing the police will do is to take statements from yourself, Ralph Fergus and Rupert Duval. Of course, they'll arrest Fergus. We'll probably advise him to give himself up this afternoon."

Mrs. Charleston said: "This is terrible."

"Not as bad as it might be," said Callaghan. "Maybe they won't charge him with murder. Possibly they'll reduce it to manslaughter. How did he sound when he telephoned you this morning?"

"He seemed quite hopeless," she said.

There was a knock on the door. Nikolls came into the office.

Callaghan said: "Hello, Windy."

Nikolls closed the door. "Well," he began, "I've seen Fergus."

"Oh! . . ." said Mrs. Charlesworth. "How is he?"

"The guy's like nothin' on earth," said Nikolls.

"What does he say?" asked Callaghan.

Nikolls said: "He practically supports everythin' she says. He says he remembers staggerin' outa the saloon after Charleston, that he hated his guts. Then he says he remembers the report of the gun. He fell over and hit his head on a stanchion. He's got a bruise on his dome like a roc's egg. The gun was in his pocket. He says he reckons it's a damned good thing that Charleston is dead."

"This is terrible," said Mrs. Charleston.

"It's not so good, is it?" said Callaghan. "Did you see Rupert Duval, Windy?"

"Yeah," said Nikolls. "He confirms what happened while he was there. He says Charleston was provoking Fergus the whole time. Duval says it got too hot for him. He couldn't stand any more of it. So he ducked. He rowed himself ashore at ten-thirty. He caught the eleven-five train back."

"I see," said Callaghan. "Well, his evidence is going to help, Mrs. Charleston. He'll be able to prove that your husband provoked Fergus."

"Poor . . . poor Ralph," said Mrs. Charleston. "This is terrible for him."

"It wasn't so good for Charleston either!" said Nikolls.

Effie Thompson knocked on the door. She came in.

"Mr. Duval is here, Mr. Callaghan," she said.

"Show him in, Effie," said Callaghan.

Mrs. Charleston looked surprised. "Did you send for Mr. Duval?" she said. "I don't understand."

"You will," said Callaghan. "Good morning, Duval."

Effie Thompson closed the door. Duval, a fair, well-built man of about forty-five, came forward.

"Good morning, Callaghan," he said casually. "Good morning, Violet, I've heard all about this. I'm so sorry for you. It's a terrible thing. I'm even more sorry for Ralph. Poor devil, he must be feeling awful. Have they arrested him yet?"

"No," said Callaghan. "And they're not going to, Duval."

"No . . .?" queried Duval.

Callaghan said: "No. Why should they arrest Fergus for something that you and Mrs. Charleston did?"

"What the devil do you mean?" said Mrs. Charleston.

Callaghan said: "A very neat little plot, Duval. But it didn't quite come off. Even the most careful criminal leaves a clue. You left three."

"Did I really?" sneered Duval. "I think you must be mad."

"What is this?" said Nikolls. "Am I dreamin' or am I dreamin'?"

"Listen, Duval," said Callaghan, "and see how mad I am. Let me give you my ideas as to what happened last night." He took out his cigarette case, lit a cigarette. Then he went on: "First of all, I should like to tell you that Nikolls here has been making some enquiries this morning. Whilst Ralph Fergus is known to have been in love with Mrs. Charleston for years, perhaps it's a coincidence that during the last two or three months she's been spending most of her time with you."

"Nonsense," said Duval.

Callaghan went on: "Charleston had made up his mind to leave his wife, that he was going to cut off her income. That didn't suit her or you. You, neither of you, have any money of your own. So Ralph Fergus—the man who loved her—was to be the fall guy. He was to be the victim of the plot you two hatched. You knew that he'd threaten Charleston. Charleston was in such a state of mind that he wrote me a letter asking me to come and see him. My job was to protect him against Fergus.

"You knew, Mrs. Charleston, that he was sending me that letter. So you made your plan. You arranged the dinner party. You knew it was impossible for your husband and Fergus to sit at the same table without quarrelling. You knew they'd both get drunk during the course of the evening. Possibly you did your best to make the situation worse than it was.

"Then Duval here carefully arranged his alibi. He took one of the Paloma dinghies and rowed ashore. Directly he was gone you brought things to a head between your husband and Fergus. They'd both drunk too much to know what they were doing. Your husband left the saloon and went to his cabin. You probably asked Fergus to go after him and bring him back. But what had happened in the meantime?

"Duval, having reached the shore, went into the little coppice at the end of the landing stage, undressed—he had a swimming suit under his clothes—and swam back to the Paloma. He carried something with him—an automatic pistol. In order to keep it dry he wrapped it in a rubber tobacco pouch.

"When your husband reached his cabin, and when Fergus was staggering along the passageway after him, Duval was hidden in the cupboard on the other side of your husband's cabin. He had wrapped himself in the dressing gown he found there. That's why the inside of it was damp. He heard the crash as Fergus fell over in the passageway. Then he shot your husband and prepared to return the same way as he had come."

Mrs. Charleston face was ghastly. "It isn't true," she said. "It isn't true."

"Keep your mouth shut, Violet," snarled Duval.

Callaghan went on: "There's no need for you to say anything. The facts are there. One thing was worrying you, Duval. You knew that Mrs. Charleston was going to plant on Fergus the automatic he'd used in the pistol shooting match—another idea of yours. You were worried about the fact that the bullet which killed Charleston was fired from a different gun, that the police check-up would prove—if they found the bullet—that the shot that killed Charleston was not fired from the pistol Fergus had. So you skewered the bullet out of the woodwork of the bunk where it had lodged. Then you swam back to the shore, dressed, caught the eleven-five back to London, leaving Fergus—who knew only that he hated Charleston, that he wanted to kill him—to carry the baby. It was easy for Mrs. Charleston to plant the gun in his pocket.

"She rowed him ashore, told him he had killed Charleston, told him to try and make a getaway, that she'd do everything she could to help him. Then she went back to the yacht and waited for me to arrive."

Mrs. Charleston shrugged her shoulders. "Well, Rupert," she said, "he's been too good for us. It didn't come off, after all."

Effie Thompson came into the office. She said: "Mr. Callaghan, there are two police officers here."

"Show them in, Effie. And, Effie . . ."

"Yes, Mr. Callaghan . . .?"

Callaghan said: "Get on to Mr. Fergus. Give him my compliments. Tell him he didn't kill Eustace Charleston after all."

Effie Thompson stood to one side as the two detective officers came into the room.

9

THE MAN WITH TWO WIVES

Effie Thompson stood with her back to the door. She asked: "Will you see her now?"

Callaghan said: "Yes, Effie. I'm curious about her. I like to see my clients—not merely to listen to them over the telephone or to read letters from them which conceal more than they say."

Effie nodded. She said: "Well . . . you'll certainly like to see this one. She may not be young but she's got something!"

"What does she look like, Effie?" asked Callaghan.

"I think she's a honey," said Effie. "She's about forty-five—but quite charming. She's got appeal too. Also she knows how to pick and wear clothes. She's a very attractive woman. If I were a man I'd fall for her."

Callaghan grinned. He said: "I can hardly wait. Show her into the office."

Mrs. Perrine came into the office. Callaghan looked her over casually. He thought he agreed with Effie. He said: "Sit down, Mrs. Perrine. Smoke a cigarette." He passed the box. "Now, listen to me. We've done our damnedest but we can't find this husband of yours. Candidly, I'm not surprised. The information you gave us wasn't very good, was it? It didn't give us much to work on. That's why I wanted to see you personally. I like to see my clients. Telephones and letters have their disadvantages, Mrs. Perrine.

"I asked you to come in this morning because I thought possibly you might be able to add to the information you've already given us." He grinned at her pleasantly.

"Frankly, between you, me and the doorpost, have you told me the truth, the whole truth, and nothing but the truth?"

She hesitated. She said: "Haven't you found out anything?"

Callaghan said: "Nothing. I've had my best assistant—Windemere Nikolls—working on this job for two weeks. He hasn't turned up a thing."

She said: "Mr. Callaghan. I've been thinking things over. I haven't given you a square deal. I haven't been quite frank with you."

Callaghan nodded. "The man who said that everybody ought to tell the whole truth to their doctor and lawyer was only half right," he said. "If you're going to employ a private detective, it's just a waste of money—if you hold out on him. So, Mrs. Perrine, I suggest you give it to me-all of it. That will be best for you—in the long run."

She said: "I ought to have told you that I know Rupert was very fond of a girl before he married me—a blonde. She was good-looking—quite a nice girl, I believe."

"What did she look like?" Callaghan asked.

"She was tall, with a beautiful figure—a natural blonde, blue eyes, a small *retroussé* nose, very tiny feet and hands." She smiled a little cynically. "Rupert would have married her, I think, if she'd had any money," she said.

Callaghan asked: "Where is this girl living—do you know? And what's her name?"

"Her name's Enid Crask," said Mrs. Perrine. "She used to live in Manchester, but I believe during the last six months she came to London. She lived somewhere just outside."

Callaghan said: "What do you mean—you believe? How did you know that?"

She said: "Just before Rupert disappeared he spent a lot of evenings away from home. He'd leave about seven and return somewhere about eleven or twelve. So he couldn't have gone far, and there were blonde hairs on his coat."

"I see," said Callaghan. "That's not bad deduction, Mrs. Perrine. You'd make a good detective yourself. By the way, have you got that note he left for you? If you have, let me look at it."

She opened her bag, handed the envelope to Callaghan. He took out a typewritten letter, read it:

Somewhere in England.

Dear Evelyn,

As far as I'm concerned, it's all over. I'm going to leave you.

I'm not even going to make any excuse for myself. I'm the lowest thing on earth. You've been much too good to me, especially when it must have been pretty obvious to you that I must have married you for your money. You know I must have money.

That's been the whole trouble with me—all my life. I must have money—and my second fault is I'm too fond of women. Shall we say I worship feminine beauty en masse. Candidly, that's why I've had so much money from you during the last six months. I've had a hell of a lot, haven't I? I suppose in my own funny way I'm sorry.

Naturally you'll have guessed that I'm keen on some girl. In point of fact I'm going to clear out with her and try and make the best of a bad job. Think as decently of me as you can. Not that I think decently of myself. I don't. I'm a thoroughly bad hat and I know it.

Yours,

Rupert.

Callaghan put the letter back in the envelope. He lit a cigarette.

"There is something else, Mr. Callaghan," said Mrs. Perrine. "I was going through Rupert's desk yesterday. A piece of paper had slipped down over the edge of a drawer. It was caught between the desk and the side of a drawer. There was an address written on it. I wondered . . ."

Callaghan said: "Let's try it, anyway. Have you got it?"

"Here it is," she said. She handed over a small torn piece of paper. On it were written the words *"Acacia Dene, Glen Road, Surbiton."*

Callaghan put it in his pocket. He said: "It's a pity you haven't a photograph of your husband. Tell me again what he's like."

She said: "You couldn't mistake Rupert. He's of middle height, slim, fair, with grey eyes and a humorous mouth. He'd stand out anywhere."

"Maybe he would—to you," said Callaghan. "You're still fond of him, aren't you? You still think of him as well as you can in spite of what he's done to you. And you still think he looks good." He grinned. "Probably I'd think he looks lousy." He got up. "All right, Mrs. Perrine, you go home and relax. We'll let you know something when we can."

She said: "It's all very well to talk about relaxing, but women are strange things, Mr. Callaghan."

Callaghan said: "You're telling me! But why particularly in this case?"

She said: "Believe it or not. I'm the sort of person who'd stand for anything from him. I just love him, that's all. Do you know I'm so fond of that fascinating blackguard that even now I find myself worrying about him, hoping he'll have enough money to go where he wants, and do what he wants, with this new woman of his."

Callaghan said: "I think you're marvelous. But don't worry about him. He's no good to you. With a face, figure and appeal like you have, Mrs. Perrine, there'll be somebody else."

She said as she went out: "Not for me, Mr. Callaghan."

Callaghan pulled the car into the side of the road. Nikolls was leaning up against the telephone booth smoking a cigarette. When Callaghan came over he said: "Don't worry, Slim. This is the boyo all right. We got him now."

Callaghan said: "Tell me about it."

Nikolls said: "It's stickin' outa foot one wife wasn't enough for this guy—he has to have two. Listen, he's livin' at this place Acacia Dene with the baby Mrs. Perrine told you about—the blonde. But his name isn't Perrine here. Oh no! They're Mr. and Mrs. Stanford. They've been married for years. They came from Manchester. Got it? It's easy, ain't it? This guy is stuck on this blonde dame but she's got no money. So he's gonna have it both ways. He marries the blonde baby up in Manchester—that's for love, see? Then he comes down to London, meets the other one an' marries her in the name of Perrine. That way he has the blonde an' the use of the Perrine money. Nice goin', hey?"

Callaghan nodded. "Not so good for our client, though," he said. "If this is right, then he's *not* married to Mrs. Perrine. It was a bigamous marriage. Well, maybe she'll stand for that as well."

Nikolls said: "She's stuck on this guy, hey? Ain't it marvelous how nice dames fall for bad guys? Maybe they like them that way. Well, where do we go from here?"

Callaghan threw his cigarette stub away. He said: "I'm tired of this case. I'm going to have a showdown. Let's go along and see Perrine."

"O.K.," said Nikolls. "I hope he's in!"

Perrine stood with his back to the fireplace looking at Callaghan. The blonde, gracefully demure, sat in the corner. Nikolls leaned against the sideboard, smoking a Lucky Strike.

Callaghan said: "Don't let's beat about the bush, Perrine, or Stanford, or whatever your name is. I think I've got you taped."

Perrine smiled. Callaghan was thinking that he matched exactly Mrs. Perrine's description of him—of medium height, graceful, fair, with smiling grey eyes and a humorous mouth. An attractive blackguard, thought Callaghan.

"So you've got me taped, Mr. Callaghan," he said. "Well, so what!"

Callaghan said: "That's what is troubling me. I don't quite know what to do."

Perrine smiled. "Perhaps I could help," he said, "especially if I knew your theory—or haven't you one?"

Callaghan said: "I've got a theory all right. I'll tell you what it is. You met Mrs. Perrine down here in London. She's an attractive woman and she had a lot of money. You wanted money. Maybe you told your blonde girl friend here that the idea would be for you to marry Mrs. Perrine, and you could both live on her income. But I don't think she liked it. It would have made her feel too small and look too small. She wanted to make a certainty of you. So she got you to marry her first. It tied you both up to each other as tight as you could be tied. You were in fact accessories to the bigamous marriage which followed to Mrs. Perrine.

"Well, you stuck it as long as you could, and then it got too much for you. Maybe your first wife here didn't like the idea of sharing you with another woman, or maybe you'd got enough of Mrs. Perrine's money salted away to want to get out and have a good time of your own. So you played it the easiest way. You sent that typewritten note to Mrs. Perrine saying you were getting out. You knew that she was crazy about you, that she'd stand for anything from you, that she wouldn't bring a charge of bigamy. Now I suppose you're going to pack up and get out of the country. Well, how's that for a case?"

Perrine said: "It's a damned good case. You needn't worry any more. It's correct. And once more—so what!" He smiled. "It looks as if we hold the trump cards in this game, doesn't it? Mind you, I'm sorry for Evelyn."

Nikolls said: "Ain't he just too sweet! He's sorry for her! Me . . . I'd like to take a poke at that fascinatin' pan of his."

The blonde said casually: "Shut up, Repulsive. Start any rough stuff here and I'll crown you with the poker."

Nikolls sighed. He began to hum a song called *"Nice People Have Nice Manners."*

Perrine said: "Well, what do you propose to do? If you're, going to apply for a warrant for bigamy you'll have to get a ripple on. We're leaving here first thing in the morning."

Callaghan said: "You needn't worry about that, Perrine. Mrs. Perrine can take it. She's got to." He lit a fresh cigarette. "You're a pretty low specimen," he went on. "I can understand everything else, but to get her to give you that open cheque for ten thousand just before you left her—that was about the meanest thing you've ever done in your life."

Perrine said: "Is that what she says?"

Callaghan nodded. "It's not only what she says, but I believe it," he said.

Perrine said: "Well, I haven't cashed the cheque yet, have I? Perhaps I didn't get a cheque. Perhaps she made that up."

Callaghan said: "Rubbish! She gave you a cheque all right, and you took it. You put it in the pocket of the body belt you wore under your shirt —she told me so." He picked up his hat. "Well, there's nothing more to be done. I'll tell Mrs. Perrine about it. If it's any consolation to you to know you've broken' up a damned nice woman's life—a woman who's played the game by you and given you a square deal. You've had a lot of her money, you've messed up her life. You're not fit to lick her shoes."

Perrine yawned. He said: "I think you're terribly touching. You'll make me cry in a minute."

Nikolls said "Slim—do me a favour. Let me take one poke at this lousy so-an'-so. Just one—"

Callaghan said: "Don't bother, Windy. Come on. This place stinks."

He went out. Nikolls followed him. Twenty yards down the road, Nikolls said: "Say, what is this?"

Callaghan said: "Pipe down, Windy. It's just getting dark. If we turn down one of these side streets, we can get round on the other side of the back garden to Acacia Dene. There's a thick hedge there."

Nikolls said: "Say, I don't get it . . ."

Callaghan said: "You don't have to."

They walked for some minutes in silence, turned down the side road, made a circle, came up behind the thick hedge. Parting the thick leaves with his hands, Callaghan could look across the lawn of Acacia Dene towards the back of the house and the garage. After a while Perrine came out. He walked to the garage, unlocked the door, went inside.

Callaghan lit a cigarette. It was almost dark now. He looked at his watch, saw they had waited twenty minutes. He said: "Come on, Windy." He walked to the back gateway, pushed it open. He crossed the lawn, went towards the garage, with Nikolls at his heels. When they got there, Callaghan said quietly: "Take a run at that garage door and burst it open. It's not too strong. It's locked."

Nikolls said: "O.K." He moved back half a dozen yards, took a run at the door, flung his bulk against it. The folding doors smashed open inwards.

Perrine, on the far side of the garage, dropped the spade.

Callaghan said: "Nice work, Stanford. Too bad you fell for that cheque business. So that's where you buried Perrine?"

Stanford leaned up against the garage wall, his face was grey.

Callaghan said: "It's damned funny. Everybody thought what you wanted them to think. You knew Rupert Perrine was leaving Mrs. Perrine. You also knew he was stuck on your blonde wife, had been paying her surreptitious visits. I imagine you've been blackmailing him for months— that's where: Mrs. Perrine's money has been going to. Then I suppose he got fed up with it. He'd had enough. He was going to talk. He was going to tell Mrs. Perrine.

"So the pair of you concocted a nice little plot. It was easy, wasn't it? Both you and Perrine were of medium height. Both of you were fair, and you'd elicited the fact from Perrine that there was no photograph of him in existence. So you killed him. You buried him there under the garage floor. Then you wrote that typewritten note to Mrs. Perrine, purporting to come from him, saying you were going to clear out. She knew he'd been keen on your wife in the old days in Manchester, but what she didn't know was that you'd married her since.

"I never guessed a thing till I saw you. You're a pretty dominant sort of person, aren't you, Stanford? I wondered why it was that nicely set as you were, with two attractive wives—one with a lot of money, you had to walk out on the rich one in order to go off with the poor one with whom you'd been living for years."

Callaghan grinned. He lit a fresh cigarette. "The idea occurred to me while I was talking to you," he said. "I thought it was just a chance, but I thought I'd test it. So I told you the phoney story about the open cheque for ten thousand pounds in the belt under Perrine's shirt. Well, you never looked there after you'd killed him, did you? So you came out here to do it now, and to get that cheque before you scrammed to-morrow."

Nikolls said: "For cryin' out loud! What a sweet little boyo it is."

Callaghan threw away his cigarette. He said: "Go on digging, Stanford. Maybe you'll have got down to him by the time Nikolls comes back with the police."

Some beads of sweat stood out on Stanford's forehead. He began to talk thickly.

He said: "Look . . ."

Callaghan said: "Save it for the judge and jury. Windy, telephone the police. There's a 'phone in the sitting-room, in the corner. Be careful of Mrs. Stanford. She might get tough."

Nikolls said: "Yeah . . . I only hope she does." He went out.

Callaghan said to Stanford: "I told you to go on digging. Get on with it. You wouldn't like to get hurt, would you? And I'd like nothing better than an excuse to beat you up."

Stanford ran his tongue over his dry lips. He picked up the spade.

10

THE LADY IN TEARS

WINDEMERE Nikolls, Callaghan's Canadian assistant, had prophesied on more than one occasion that some woman would be the undoing of Callaghan Investigations. Each time that some lovely lady in a jam had come to consult Callaghan, Nikolls had cocked a wary eye at Effie Thompson, had wondered whether this was going to be the one. On each of these occasions the words "I told you so" had been waiting to be uttered. But somehow Callaghan's luck had held and Nikolls had breathed again, until Mrs. Geralda Vaile arrived upon the scene. Then Nikolls knew that Callaghan was for it. He knew that this time there was no way out.

It was one of those pitch black nights, in which war-time London specialized, that Mr. Callaghan came out of the Green Melon Club—where for two hours he had been consuming double whiskies and sodas and pondering on the uncertainties of the private detective business—switched on his torch and began to make his way towards his office and flat in Berkeley Square.

It was close on twelve o'clock—a quiet hour in those days—and, as Callaghan turned into the narrow street running into Park Lane, he heard a sound that caused him to switch off his electric torch and stand quite still, listening.

Definitely, thought Callaghan, he heard the sound of a woman sobbing, then a soft but intense feminine voice said "Damn!" Then there were more sobs emanating,

Callaghan thought, from the same female, then a final and conclusive "Damn!"

He switched on his torch, turned it in the direction of the last "Damn" and came to the conclusion that his theory was correct. It was a lady, and the tears were due neither to sentiment, pity nor unhappiness, but to sheer unmitigated anger.

She stood—a slim, extremely well-dressed and chic figure—clutching a cigarette lighter which refused to work—in a small gloved hand. The light from Callaghan's torch sweeping upwards showed that she was beautiful as well as graceful. She looked at him warily as he moved towards her.

Callaghan took off his black soft hat. He said: "Obviously, something's wrong. But it's not too wrong, otherwise you wouldn't be damning it as well as crying about it. Can I help?"

She produced a smile. The smile, Callaghan thought, was quite delightful. It also showed a perfect set of teeth.

She said: "I'm fearfully sorry you heard me using such language but what could I do? I live in the house on the corner of this street and Park Lane. My people are away and I've given our two remaining old servants the evening off. So there's nobody in. In the circumstances you can imagine how I loved dropping my front door key in the gutter ten minutes ago. Since then my torch battery has given out and my lighter won't work. I've been wandering about trying to find the thing by groping—just look at my gloves! Wouldn't you be angry?"

"Definitely," said Callaghan. "I'd probably have used much worse language than you did. Possibly I should have had a good cry too. Anyhow, all's well now, and my suggestion is that you sit down, on my raincoat, on this rather convenient doorstep and smoke a cigarette while I try and discover the missing key."

She said: "I think you're heaven-sent—definitely! Thank you very much."

Callaghan took off his raincoat, put it on the doorstep, gave her a cigarette, lit it for her, proceeded to search for the key. He was amused. The idea of Mr. Callaghan of Callaghan Investigations being heaven-sent was, he thought, almost too good to be true.

After five minutes concentrated effort he found the key. She stubbed out her cigarette, got up, picked up his raincoat and handed it to him with a charming smile.

She said: "Thank you so very much. I think you're very nice."

Callaghan said: "You'd be surprised!" He handed her the key. He went on: "I think I'd better see you to your door. You've no torch and you might drop that key again."

They walked down the street. At the end she stopped at the front entrance of an imposing house. She said: "This is my home and thank you once again." She held out the key to Callaghan, who mounted the steps, opened the front door for her and stood aside for her to enter. She took the key from him, gave his hand a little squeeze. She said: "You've been very good and kind. And I think you're a sweet! Good night!"

She disappeared into the house. The door closed quietly.

Callaghan walked away slowly. He concluded that there was a certain allure about this lady. He was even more amused at the idea of being "a sweet." Very few people thought that Mr. Callaghan was "a sweet." Many of them in fact thought *very* differently!

He walked back to the Green Melon Club—which had won medals and probably still does for breaking the licensing law regarding closing hours—and drank another whisky and soda.

Two days afterwards, in the afternoon, as Callaghan was finishing his tea, Effie Thompson came into the office. She said: "Mr. Callaghan, there's a lady to see you. I think you'd like to see her. She's very beautiful and won't give her name."

Callaghan grinned. He said: "Show her in, Effie. All our best cases have been beautiful. And don't look so acid about it."

Effie Thompson went away. She returned in a few minutes, ushered the client into Callaghan's room.

He got up. He said: "Well . . . well . . . well . . .! Who was it said that the world was a small place?" He placed a chair for her in front of his desk, went back to his own chair, sat down, looking at her.

She said: "Isn't this extraordinary? If only I'd known the other evening that the very kind person who found my key for me was the great Mr. Callaghan himself . . .!"

Callaghan smiled at her. He said: "I thought you were very lovely the other night, but I hadn't a real chance of looking at you. You're quite marvelous. By the way, what's the trouble? Have you lost your key again?"

She shook her head. "It's rather more serious," she said. "I'd better tell you the whole story. Then you can tell me if you'll help me."

Callaghan offered her a cigarette, leaned across the desk, lit it and one for himself. "I'm all attention," he said.

"I'm Mrs. Geralda Vaile," she began. "I was married four years ago to Arthur Vaile. He's an impossible person and I propose to leave him shortly and begin divorce proceedings against him. Incidentally, I was foolish enough to tell him so and it hasn't made me any more popular with him. At the moment he's actively disliking me. Do you understand all that, Mr. Callaghan?"

Callaghan nodded.

"You know where we live," she continued. "Well . . . in the safe in the library on the second floor is my mother's diamond tiara. It's the only valuable thing I've got. Arthur knows that I propose to take it away with me and he's watching me like a cat. He doesn't intend that I shall have it. He'd do anything to keep it. That's where you come in."

"Yes?" said Callaghan. "Tell me how I come in?"

"I propose," she went on, "to telephone Arthur this evening, ask him to dine with me at The Splendide to discuss amicably the divorce. He'll come. He'll think that he can talk me out of it. Whilst we are dining you slip round to the house, go in—I'll give you a key—go to the safe in the library, open it—I'll give you the combination—get the tiara and hand it over to me. When Arthur gets home it will be gone and he won't be able to do anything about it. It's my property."

Callaghan said: "He wouldn't be able to do anything about it anyhow—a married man cannot bring action against his wife for the removal by her of his property while she is domiciled with him. Even if the tiara belonged to him you'd still be safe."

"That's as maybe," she said. "But it's mine and I want it. Will you get it for me, Mr. Callaghan?"

Callaghan looked at her. He thought she was very lovely, and, as Windemere Nikolls is fond of pointing out, he has a very soft spot where beautiful women are concerned.

He nodded casually. He said: "I'll try anything once. Now about the safe combination . . ."

She said: "Just a moment please, Mr. Callaghan. Business is business." She opened her handbag, produced a packet of banknotes, put them on the desk in front of him.

"That's your fee," she said with a charming smile. "It's two hundred and fifty pounds. It's not enough but at least it's something. And one day"—she looked at him demurely—"I might be able to do something for you."

"Who knows?" said Callaghan. He smiled back at her. Both of them seemed to like it. Then she began to laugh.

She said: "Now, Mr. Callaghan, shall we talk about the safe combination . . .?"

Next morning, Callaghan, seated at his desk, experienced one of those glows of self-satisfaction which went with the sunlit day. After all, she was a very lovely person. She had her tiara and he, Callaghan, had two hundred and fifty pounds. He concluded the detective business wasn't so bad after all.

And then it happened. Windemere Nikolls came into Callaghan's office, a newspaper in one hand and what was intended to be a dramatic sort of grin about his mouth. Callaghan, looking at him, thought that it was the sort of grin which said as near as a grin could "I told you so!"

Nikolls said: "Well, it looks as if you won it this time, Slim. I always reckoned one of these fine days you was goin' to run yourself into a bundle of trouble with some dame. Well, it's happened all right." He put the newspaper on Callaghan's desk and pointed with a fat forefinger to a news story. Callaghan read it. The news story said in fact that the night before, a valuable tiara—the property of the Countess of Hawyck—had been stolen from her house in Park Lane, that the robbery had been carried out in the most expert manner, that somebody had the combination of the safe and as key to the house and had selected a moment when the family were away and the servants not at home.

Callaghan looked at Nikolls. He said: "It's not quite so good, is it, Windy?"

Windy said: "Nope. It certainly is not. In point of fact it might be goddam bad." He looked at Callaghan wryly. "You know, if Gringall at the Yard got an idea about this," he went on, "I wonder what he wouldn't do to you."

Callaghan said: "Quite! No one of course would believe what really happened. They certainly would not believe it if I told them the truth." A picture flashed through his mind—a picture of the charm of the lady when he had handed over the tiara to her, or her promise to come and see him soon.

He grinned sourly. She'd be coming along soon—like hell she would!

He got up, put on his hat. He said to Nikolls: "I'm going out. I'll be back this afternoon maybe."

Nikolls grinned. He said: "Yeah? You're not feelin' so good, are you, Slim? But it's no good thinkin' about it. If I was you I'd go out an' have a drink."

Callaghan said darkly: "What the hell do you think I'm going to do? I'm going to have a lot of drinks."

He went out of the office. As he closed the outer door, Effie Thompson, her red head bent over her typewriter, heard him mutter something about what he would like to do to that woman.

The third act in this rather peculiar drama happened at four-fifteen on the same afternoon. Callaghan, seated at his desk and immersed in the details of a case which concerned a Cement Company who were missing quite a lot of petty cash, raised his head. Nikolls came into the office, an expression of the most intense amazement on his face.

He said: "Don't look now, but believe it or not she's here."

Callaghan tensed, sat back in his chair. He said: "What!"

Nikolls said: "She's here—Mrs. Vaile! She wants to see you. What d'you know about that for nerve? I'll say this baby's good. An' is she a looker?" He whistled. "Boy—she has certainly got somethin'."

Callaghan said: "Ask her to come in. And you'd better stay here."

A minute afterwards she came into the room. She was dressed quietly and in the most exquisite taste. She was fresh, smiling, completely adorable. Callaghan looked at her in amazement, then he got up, put a chair for her in front of his desk, went back to his own seat.

He said: "I think you have the most superb nerve in the world and—"

She put up a small gloved hand. She said: "Dear Mr. Callaghan, there isn't any necessity to get excited. Surely my best guarantee of good faith is the fact that I have come back to see you." She threw him a bewitching smile. "I said I'd come back, didn't I? And here I am."

Callaghan said: "So I see. You realize exactly what you've done, don't you? By a very clever trick and by appealing to the better side of my nature—and there's no need for you to grin, Windy, when I talk about the better side of my nature—you persuaded me to be an innocent accessory to stealing the Countess of Hawyck's diamond tiara. In other words, if the police get wise to this what do you think is going to happen to me? Do you think they'd believe my story?"

She shook her head. She said softly: "No, of course they wouldn't. But, dear Mr. Callaghan, there isn't the slightest possibility of anything happening to you. I give you my word. You see I have everything organized. I am taking care of everything—as the Americans say—even Mr. Callaghan."

Callaghan said: "Well, I'll be damned."

"Possibly," she said sweetly, "but not by me. Now listen to me. You have, as you have said, become an innocent accessory to the stealing of the Hawyck tiara. I have it. Well, I think you'll agree with me that to dispose of it would be very difficult. I am informed by a friend of mine who is a great expert that if the tiara were broken up its value would be greatly lessened. As a piece of jewellery it is so well known that it is obviously impossible to get rid of it in the open market, and if one were to try to sell it to a fence one would receive practically nothing for it. And my work, and"—she flashed another delightful smile at him—"your work would have been in vain. I have another and better idea, Mr. Callaghan, and I have come here to ask you to help me again."

Callaghan looked at her, his mouth slightly open. He was speechless. Nikolls, leaning against the wall by the door, a cigarette hanging from the corner of his mouth, said quietly to himself: "Jeez . . .!"

Callaghan recovered his power of speech. He said, enunciating the words carefully and slowly: "So-you'd-like-me-to-help-you-again?"

She nodded. As she smiled, he saw the flash of her perfect teeth.

He said: "What a hope you've got, Mrs.—or Miss—Vaile—or whatever your name is."

She said: "Exactly, Mr. Callaghan—my name is Vaile and my Christian name is Geralda. If you'd like to call me Geralda you may. I like all my friends to call me by my first name."

Callaghan said wearily: "Very well, Geralda. Go on, I like listening to you. So I'm going to help you again, am I?"

She said brightly: "Oh yes. You see you've got to."

Callaghan said: "What the hell do you mean?"

"Now don't get angry," she said in a soothing voice. "First of all listen to my idea. I have told you that it would be very inconvenient at the moment to get rid of the

Hawyck tiara by any means legal or illegal, but there is one excellent idea which occurred to me right from the beginning. In point of fact," she went on, "I had it before I waited for you to leave the Green Melon Club so that I could lose my key and you could find it. I had the idea then. I'll tell you what it is.

"I am given to understand that tomorrow the assessors of the Insurance Company who insured the Hawyck tiara will publish the usual notice in *The Times*. In other words, Mr. Callaghan—or may I call you Slim, I believe all your friends do—the assessors will offer a reward of one-tenth of the value of the tiara to anyone giving information which will lead to its recovery." She smiled demurely at Callaghan.

He sat looking at her. Nikolls made a little hissing noise through his teeth.

"I should also tell you," she went on, "that the Hawyck tiara is insured for one hundred and twenty thousand pounds. So all you have to do is to give the assessors information which will lead to its recovery and you receive twelve thousand pounds. Now what is more normal," she went on, "than that a very clever private detective like Mr. Callaghan should by some odd chance find out who had this tiara? What would be more normal than he should go to the Insurance Company and tell them about it—more especially, Mr. Callaghan, when I tell you that the tiara was insured by the International & Consolidated Insurance Company, for whom I am informed you have done quite a lot of work. In point of fact, it is really an ideal situation, and all you have to do is to collect the twelve thousand pounds, to give me eleven thousand

and to keep one thousand for your own services, and everybody will be absolutely happy."

Callaghan said grimly: "I must congratulate you on an extremely clever scheme." His sense of humour was reasserting itself. He looked at her and grinned. He said: "You've certainly got brains in that head of yours, Geralda. There was some very clever planning behind all this."

She said softly: "My friends have always said I was clever, Mr. Callaghan. But," she went on modestly, "I've never really believed them until now."

He said: "And supposing I refuse?"

She looked at him. "Oh, no," she said. "You wouldn't refuse, Mr. Callaghan. You won't refuse. You see you couldn't refuse."

Callaghan said: "No? Why not?"

She said: "I'll tell you. If you don't do what I want you to do I'm going to write an anonymous letter to Scotland Yard and tell them that whilst they were unable to check up the fingerprints on the safe from which the tiara was removed—because those prints were not recorded at Scotland Yard—if they will take Mr. Slim Callaghan's prints they will find they match up and that he was the person who removed the tiara."

She looked at him seriously. She said: "You know it would hurt me very much, Slim, to have to do a thing like that."

Callaghan said nothing. He looked at Nikolls. Nikolls, Callaghan saw, was breathing very heavily. He looked as if he might have a stroke at any moment. Callaghan leaned over, opened the cigarette box on his desk, selected a cigarette, lit it. Then he said brusquely: "Well, there's only one thing to be done. I know when I'm beaten. All right, I'll do it. As you say, it's a perfect set-up. I have worked for the International & Consolidated Insurance Company. It is on the cards that information would come to me as to where a valuable mixing piece of jewellery might be. It is normal that I should go to them. They'll be so glad to get the damned thing back they won't ask any questions. You know that too.

"I'll do it, but," he went on, "I want nothing out of it. They'll pay the ten per cent reward of twelve thousand pounds and that will be handed to you. So there's only one thing to be done."

She said: "Yes, what is that, Slim?"

He said: "You bring the tiara here."

She shook her head. "I couldn't do that, Slim," she said. "I really couldn't. And it isn't because I don't trust you. I do trust you, but," she went on, "I'm not going to hand that tiara over to you until you give me the money. I want my eleven thousand pounds first."

Callaghan looked at her a trifle wearily. He said: "You know all the answers, Geralda, don't you? Very well, I'll see the Insurance people tomorrow. You'd better meet me on the morning of the day afterwards—Thursday—at twelve-thirty. We'll meet in the lounge of the Hotel Splendide. I shall have the money and I want the tiara."

She said: "But of course. It's going to be quite wonderful, isn't it, Slim? The whole thing seems so awfully legal—you know, no risk at all. Well, I must be going now. You are a dear, aren't you, to help me like this?" She got up. "Till Thursday morning," she said, "at twelve-thirty at the Splendide. Good-bye, Slim. Good-bye, dear Mr. Nikolls."

She walked gracefully out of the office. Nikolls heard the outer door close and pushed himself away from the wall. He looked at Callaghan almost miserably.

He said: "Well . . . for cryin' out loud . . .!"

Windemere Nikolls was pained to observe that Callaghan spent most of Tuesday evening drinking in the company of no less a person than Mr. Blooey Stevens who, being of criminal tendencies, was, thought Nikolls, no proper company for his chief at the moment.

On the Wednesday, Callaghan did not even appear at the office. Nikolls wondered why. Maybe, he thought, the boss was getting a hangover. Maybe he was too burned up to concentrate on business.

Callaghan's assistant considered Mrs. Geralda Vaile with a scowl. Well . . . he'd always said it would happen one day. If you got mixed up with good-lookin' dames and fell for their stories you just had to pay the bill and grin—if you would. Still, it was very tough.

That Callaghan would go through with the business was obvious. He had to. There was no way out. He was between the devil and the deep sea.

He appeared at the office at half-past eleven on the Thursday morning. Nikolls, who was sitting in the big armchair smoking, got lugubriously to his feet.

He said: "Well, Slim . . . how is it? Did the Company pay up?"

Callaghan nodded. "They paid up," he said. "I've got the cheque. I've promised to return the tiara to them to-morrow."

Nikolls nodded. "Well," he said glumly. "I hope you get it. I hope she don't try anything else." He stopped talking when he saw the expression on Callaghan's face.

Callaghan looked through his post, lit a cigarette, picked up his hat. He said: "Come on . . . let's get this business over. You'd better come too."

"Yeah," said Nikolls, "I had. Just in case that snappy number tries to steal your wristwatch!"

When they arrived in the lounge at the Splendide, she was awaiting them. She wore a neat tailored suit, carried a slim handbag. There was no sign of the tiara.

Callaghan said: "Good morning. You're very punctual. I hope you're feeling well."

She flashed a smile at him. "I'm feeling wonderful," she said. "And I hope you are, and you, Mr. Nikolls. By the way, have you got the money, Slim dear?"

Callaghan said: "Yes . . . I've got a bearer cheque from the International &: Consolidated. I've promised to return the tiara to-morrow. Where is it?"

She looked at him. "Slim dear," she said sadly. "I'm sorry you think I'm so stupid. You really didn't think I was going to take a cheque, did you? Why . . . supposing I handed you the tiara and took the cheque . . . well, an order might have been made to stop payment, mightn't it? Or I might be arrested in the Bank whilst I was trying to cash it. No, Slim . . . I must have cash."

Callaghan said wearily: "Very well, I'll cash the cheque myself—the International & Consolidated Bank is just along the street. But where's the tiara?"

She smiled at him. "I'll come along with you," she said. "And I'll wait outside the Bank . . . but on the other side of the street, with Mr. Nikolls. You cash the cheque and I promise you that when you hand me my eleven thousand pounds you shall have the tiara within twenty seconds."

Callaghan said: "You think of everything, don't you!"

They walked down Piccadilly. When they were twenty yards from the Bank she said: "Now Mr. Nikolls and I will cross over here and wait for you, Slim. Please be quick. I've so much to do to-day!"

Callaghan said nothing. She crossed the road escorted by Nikolls. Callaghan went into the Bank. Five minutes later he came out. He crossed the road and joined them. In his hands were several packets of notes. He handed them to her.

She said: "Thank you, Slim. And now for the tiara."

She turned and waved her hand. A sleek car shot out from the pavement fifty yards away and drove slowly towards them. It stopped and a hand holding a small parcel came out through the driving window. She took the parcel, handed it to Callaghan. "You'd better look at it," she said, "just to see you've got the real thing."

Callaghan tore off the paper wrapping at one end. He examined the contents. He said: "O.K."

"*Au revoir*, Slim," she said. She gave him a sweet smile, the door of the car opened. In a split second she was inside and the car was speeding towards the Park.

Callaghan lit a cigarette. He said to Nikolls: "Let's go back to the office."

Callaghan opened the wrapping and put the Hawyck tiara on the desk. The sunlight reflected on the superb stones. "A lovely piece of work," he said. "Get through to the International & Consolidated, Windy," he went on. "I want to speak to the General Manager."

"O.K.," said Nikolls. A minute afterwards he handed the receiver to Callaghan.

"Good morning, Mr. Varney," said Callaghan. "This is to let you know that I've got the tiara. I'll get into a cab and bring it down to the office right away. I expect you'll feel safer if it's in your own vault."

He hung up. Then he lit a cigarette, put his hand in the breast pocket of his coat, brought out a cheque. He handed it to Nikolls. "That's the International & Consolidated cheque for twelve thousand," he said with a grin. "Take it down to the Bank and cash it and bring the cash straight back here."

Nikolls gazed at the cheque in amazement. He muttered: "What the hell . . .?"

Callaghan said: "I knew she wouldn't take the cheque—even if it was a 'bearer' cheque. I knew she'd think I'd try and pull something. So I was ready. I went into the Bank and hung around for a few minutes and then came out again. I knew she would think I'd cashed the cheque."

Nikolls looked at him, his jaw dropping. "Well . . . what the hell did you do?" he asked.

"I didn't do anything," said Callaghan. "I had those banknotes on me when I went into the Bank. I got them from Blooey Stevens. They were very good forgeries.

All except the top ones. The top ones were her own five fifty-pound notes—the ones she gave me. She gets her two hundred and fifty pounds back. The Countess gets her tiara, and we get twelve thousand pounds. Well . . . what's the matter with that?"

Nikolls said nothing. He reached for his hat. As he went out he muttered: "Well . . . I'll be sugared an' iced. Ain't you the pip . . . ain't you the complete little pip!"

Callaghan grinned and helped himself to a cigarette.

11

THE DENCOURT STILETTO

WHEN Effie Thompson showed Mrs. Dencourt into Callaghan's office, Nikolls's face expressed open admiration. Mrs. Dencourt was a very beautiful woman.

Callaghan got up. He said: "Good morning. Won't you sit down? This is Mr. Nikolls, my Canadian assistant." He paused as Nikolls brought a chair forward, noticed the extreme grace with which she seated herself.

Then he said: "Will you tell me what it is you want to see me about, Mrs. Dencourt?"

"Mr. Callaghan, I am in terrible trouble and I want your help." There was an obvious note of agitation in her voice.

Nikolls said: "Don't worry, lady, you're goin' to get it. Nobody who looks like you do is gonna ask my help in vain."

Callaghan said: "Shut up, Windy." He opened the cigarette box on his desk, offered it to Mrs. Dencourt, lit her cigarette.

She said: "I'm Mrs. Herbert Dencourt. You've probably heard the name."

"Of course," said Callaghan. "I remember. You've just started a divorce action against your husband. And your husband, if I remember rightly, is the owner of one of the most valuable collections of jewels in this country."

She nodded. "Yes, that's what I have come to see you about—those jewels. I've stolen some of them."

Nikolls said under his breath: "Say . . . what d'you know about that! Ain't she too sweet!"

Callaghan said: "This is very interesting, Mrs. Dencourt. Tell me about it."

She leaned back in her chair. She said: "Mr. Callaghan, for years my husband has been terribly unkind to me. I was fond of him, but any love I had for him has been quite killed by his cruelty. Two or three months ago I made up my mind that as soon as possible I would leave him, that I would bring an action for divorce against him."

"I see," said Callaghan. "You didn't tell him of your plan?"

"No, I daren't. He's quite ruthless. I knew he'd do everything to make things difficult for me. And I was furious with him. I wanted to do something that would hurt him as much as possible and something that would give me some money to live on when I decided to leave him. So I got an idea."

Nikolls interrupted: "Some idea! She grabbed the family plate."

Callaghan turned to Nikolls. "Do shut up, Windy," he said. "Go on, Mrs. Dencourt."

"Amongst my husband's collection of jewellery," she continued, "is a dagger-a stiletto. It's been in the family for, hundreds of years. It's called the Dencourt stiletto. You may have heard of it. The hilt and scabbard are thickly encrusted with most precious jewels. It is valued at a hundred thousand pounds. I made up my mind that when I left Herbert I'd take that with me."

Callaghan said: "I see. How were you going to do that?"

Mrs. Dencourt went on: "I got in touch with a man named Larcomb who lived in the neighbourhood. I had heard that he was game for anything and was an expert cracksman. I gave him a key so that he could enter the house."

"Did this bozo pull the job off?" asked Nikolls.

"Yes, he got the stiletto. Three weeks after that I left my husband. I brought the action for divorce that you know about."

Callaghan asked: "Weren't you afraid that your husband would discover the theft, Mrs. Dencourt?"

"No," she replied. "The stiletto was kept with the rest of his collection in a special safe in the library. It's only opened about every six months when the pieces are taken out to be cleaned and inspected. I knew some months would elapse before the theft was discovered."

"And now what's the trouble, Mrs. Dencourt?" asked Callaghan. "You have the stiletto."

"That's the trouble, Mr. Callaghan," she said, "I haven't. The man Larcomb refuses to give it up to me. He's blackmailing me. He says he won't return it unless I pay him five thousand pounds."

Callaghan said: "You are in a jam, aren't you? It's not so good. What do you want me to do?"

She stubbed out her cigarette end in the ashtray beside her. She said: "I'm certain you could bluff Larcomb into handing back that stiletto. He's had convictions before. He's afraid of the police. If you told him that I'd got fearfully frightened about the whole business, that I wanted to return the stiletto to my husband, he'd have to hand it over."

"And do you intend to return it to your husband if we get it back, Mrs. Dencourt?" Callaghan asked.

"Yes, I suppose so," she said miserably. "I should never have taken it in the first place."

Callaghan asked: "Do you know where this Larcomb is?"

Mrs. Dencourt opened her handbag and took out a card. She handed it to Callaghan.

"Here is his address," she said.

Callaghan looked at the card for a moment, then he held it out to Nikolls. He said: "Very well. I think this is a job for you, Windy. You'd better go and see this bird Larcomb. Talk turkey to him. Tell him that unless he returns the stiletto we'll hand him over to the police."

Nikolls got up. He took the card. "O.K.," he said. "I'll talk to him."

Mrs. Dencourt looked relieved. She smiled. "I can never thank you enough, Mr. Callaghan. When do you think you'll know?"

Callaghan said: "Well, we shall move immediately. Supposing you come in to-morrow morning at eleven o'clock and see me then, Mrs. Dencourt. Perhaps we'll have some news for you."

"I'll be here at eleven," she said. "Thank you . . . thank you, Mr. Callaghan."

She held out her hand, walked to the door. Nikolls opened the door, watched her walk across the outer office, sighed as she went out. He said: "What a baby! So that's the beautiful Mrs. Dencourt. And, boy, is she beautiful! Some blonde!"

Effie Thompson appeared in the doorway. She said: "Excuse me, Mr. Callaghan. Was that Mrs. Dencourt who just went out?"

"Yes," said Callaghan. "Why, what's on your mind, Effie?"

Effie said: "Well, I may be wrong, but that woman's hair was dyed blonde, Mr. Callaghan. I'm certain of it. Mrs. Dencourt is a real blonde."

"Say," said Nikolls. "What the hell's goin' on around here?"

"Are you sure, Effie?" asked Callaghan.

"I'm absolutely certain," said Effie.

Nikolls said: "What does 'X' do now?"

"Listen, Windy," said Callaghan. "It's obvious this Mrs. Dencourt is a phoney, but there's no reason why we shouldn't go on with this business. There's something behind it. Go to the address she's given you. See this fellow Larcomb. See what happens. Get a ripple on. You'd better get off at once."

"O.K.," said Nikolls. "If I don't come back you'll know I've been sandbagged." He picked up his hat, went to the door. "Say . . . what d'ya know about that blonde!" he said as he went out.

Callaghan turned to Effie Thompson. He said: "Go through the newspaper cuttings, Effie. Find Mrs. Dencourt's address. The real Mrs. Dencourt. Get through on the telephone. Tell her I'm coming round to see her, that it's urgent."

"Very well, Mr. Callaghan," said Effie. She went back to her office.

Callaghan lit a fresh cigarette, sat blowing smoke rings. He was thinking about the woman who said she was Mrs. Dencourt.

*

It was four o'clock when Callaghan was shown into Mrs. Herbert Dencourt's sitting-room at her flat in Knightsbridge. It was a large well-furnished room, and the woman who rose to meet him was of medium height, slim and graceful.

She said: "Good afternoon, Mr. Callaghan. I was intrigued to get the telephone message from your office. I am very curious." She motioned him to a chair.

Callaghan said: "Mrs. Dencourt, I'll soon satisfy your curiosity. This morning a woman who looked something like you—but not quite so beautiful—came to my office with an extraordinary story. She said that her husband—Herbert Dencourt—had been cruel to her, that she'd made up her mind to leave him, but before she did so she decided to steal the jewel-studded stiletto which had been in the Dencourt family for years. In fact it was stolen but the man who actually committed the robbery refuses to return it to her. She asked my assistance in getting back the stiletto so that she could return it to her husband."

Mrs. Dencourt gasped. "Good heavens!" she said.

Callaghan continued: "My astute secretary, Miss Thompson, noticed that this woman's hair was dyed blonde. We guessed she was an impostor. So I rang you immediately. I thought you might be able to help us to elucidate this mystery."

"This is terrible," said Mrs. Dencourt. "But I can understand what has happened," she went on. "The woman who came to see you must have been my one-time maid—Phyllis Lane. The story she told you was in effect true. Before I left my husband I did intend to steal the Dencourt stiletto. I took my maid into my confidence and she proposed that a man called Larcomb should actually carry out the burglary. But at the last moment I changed my mind. I couldn't go through with it. I called the whole thing off. Well, there is no doubt what has happened."

Callaghan said: "You mean that your maid and this man Larcomb have done the job between them without your knowledge. I can guess the rest of the story, Mrs. Dencourt. Larcomb has the stiletto and won't part with it, and your maid is trying to bluff us into getting it back from him. Then she'll do a deal with your husband."

Mrs. Dencourt nodded. "It looks very much like that, doesn't it, Mr. Callaghan? Oh, how I wish I'd taken that stiletto myself."

Callaghan said: "You still feel that way?"

"Yes," she said. "I threw this plan overboard because I thought there was still a chance of a reconciliation with my husband, but his conduct became so appalling that two or three weeks afterwards I left him and began my action for divorce. He's making life unbearable for me. If I had that stiletto at least I should have something to bargain with."

"You're getting no money at all from him?" asked Callaghan.

"No," she said. "I think he hates me. He's a terrible man, Mr. Callaghan. Since I left him I've discovered that he's very keen on some woman he intends to marry when my divorce goes through. Oh dear, what are we to do about this? It seems an awful situation."

Callaghan said: "I don't know that it is. Listen, Mrs. Dencourt. I told the phoney Mrs. Dencourt to come back to-morrow morning at eleven o'clock to see me. I told her that in the meantime we'd try and get the stiletto returned by Larcomb. Well, she'll turn up to-morrow. We'll give her a little surprise. We'll tell her that so far as she's concerned we know the whole story." He got up. "Now I suggest you come and see me at my office to-morrow about eleven-fifteen."

She nodded. "Thank you, Mr. Callaghan," she said. "I'll do that."

Callaghan said: "Well, good-bye for the moment, Mrs. Dencourt. Don't worry too much. We'll straighten this out somehow."

He went out.

Effie Thompson was busy typing when Callaghan came into the outer office the next morning just before eleven o'clock. She said: "Good morning, Mr. Callaghan. Mr. Nikolls has just come in. He's in your office."

"What's he doing?" asked Callaghan.

Effie smiled. "I think he's picking his teeth with the Dencourt stiletto!"

Callaghan laughed. He said: "I'm glad to hear that! Effie, the woman who came yesterday and said she was Mrs. Dencourt will be here in a few moments. Show her in when she arrives. The real Mrs. Dencourt is coming at eleven-fifteen. You might show her into Nikolls's office and ask her to wait a few minutes."

Callaghan went into his own office, closed the door behind him. Nikolls was sitting in the armchair by Callaghan's desk, smoking a cigarette. He was swinging the Dencourt stiletto gently between his fingers.

Callaghan said: "Well, Windy?"

"It's in the bag," said Nikolls. "I saw this guy Larcomb last night. I told him plenty. I told him I was Chief Detective-Inspector Windemere from Scotland Yard. And did he fall for it!"

Callaghan grinned. He said: "What—with an accent like yours. He must have thought you'd come from the Police College!"

"Police College or not," said Nikolls, "he fell for it. And what do you think he did?"

"I don't know," said Callaghan.

"Well, he got the breeze up and handed over the stiletto. And here it is. You should have seen this guy's face when I told him the truth."

"Nice work," said Callaghan. He leaned over the desk, looked closely at the stiletto. "By Jove, look at those jewels," he said. "They must be worth a fortune."

At that moment Effie Thompson knocked at the door. Callaghan said quickly: "Hide that thing, Windy!"

"Mrs. Dencourt to see you, Mr. Callaghan," announced Effie.

"So the little phoney's arrived!" muttered Nikolls.

Phyllis Lane, well-turned out and with her dyed blonde hair carefully dressed, came into the office.

She said: "Good morning, Mr. Callaghan."

Callaghan said: "Good morning, Miss Lane. Sit down. I want to talk to you."

Her voice changed. She said: "Oh . . . well . . . so you're wise to me, hey?"

"I'm wise to the whole business," said Callaghan. "You should have had that hair dyed a little more successfully.

I saw Mrs. Dencourt yesterday afternoon and got the whole story."

She shrugged her shoulders. She said: "Well, you can't say I didn't try. Once I'd got that dagger I could have done a deal with Dencourt."

"I guessed that too," said Callaghan.

Effie Thompson knocked on the door. Callaghan called to her to come in. She said: "Mr. Callaghan, Mr. Herbert Dencourt's been on the telephone. He sounded fearfully angry. He gave me a message for you."

"What did he say?" asked Callaghan.

"He told me to tell you that he knows all about everything, that he received a note this morning from a man named Larcomb saying that his wife, Mrs. Dencourt, had got the Dencourt stiletto, that you were representing her. He told me to tell you that he'd be round here in ten minutes with a police officer and unless the stiletto is handed over there's going to be a lot of trouble."

Callaghan said: "Right, Effie. Thank you very much."

Phyllis Lane got up. She said: "Listen, I think I've got an appointment. This is where I get out."

"All right," said Callaghan. "You get out. And think yourself lucky you're getting away as easily as you are."

"You're telling me," she said. "So long, everybody."

She hurried through the door which Effie Thompson was holding open for her. They heard the outer office door slam as she went out.

Nikolls said: "Say, what is this? You're not letting that baby scram, are you? Why—"

Callaghan interrupted. "Shut up, Windy. I'm going to play this my way." He turned to Effie Thompson. "Has the real Mrs. Dencourt arrived yet?" he asked.

"Yes, Mr. Callaghan," said Effie.

"Bring her in," said Callaghan.

A minute later Mrs. Dencourt came into the office.

Callaghan said: "Good morning, Mrs. Dencourt. Listen, your husband will be here in a minute. We've got the stiletto. Larcomb handed it over. But he's sent a note to your husband telling him that you have the stiletto. Now will you take my word that if you do what I tell you everything will be all right?"

Mrs. Dencourt thought for a moment, then she said: "Yes, I will."

"All right," said Callaghan. "Now remember this. *You* stole the Dencourt stiletto. You stole it *yourself*. You brought it away with you when you left your husband, and since then you've *lost* it. You don't know where it is. Do you understand that, Mrs. Dencourt?"

"Yes . . . yes . . . I understand," she said.

Effie Thompson announced: "Mr. Dencourt is here, Mr. Callaghan, and Detective-Inspector Gringall."

"Show them in, Effie," said Callaghan.

Detective-Inspector Gringall walked into the office, followed by a thick-set dark man with an unpleasant scowl on his face.

Callaghan said: "Good morning, Gringall. This is Mr. Dencourt, I believe?"

Dencourt spoke in a brusque, threatening tone. "You believe correctly, Mr. Callaghan. I understand you're in league with my wife, who has the Dencourt stiletto. I give you both exactly two minutes to hand that stiletto over, or I shall place the matter in the hands of the police."

"It looks as if you've done that already, Mr. Dencourt," said Callaghan. "Sit down. Sit down, Inspector."

Nikolls said: "Yeah. Take your weight off your feet."

"Well . . ." began Dencourt again. "What about it . . .?"

Callaghan said: "Don't get excited, Dencourt, you really must try to control yourself."

"My God . . .!" said Dencourt furiously.

Callaghan looked at him coldly. He said: "Shut up, Dencourt, before I have you thrown out." He turned to Gringall. "Now, Inspector, exactly what is it you want?"

Gringall said: "Well, Mr. Callaghan, Mr. Dencourt here complains that the Dencourt stiletto has been stolen."

"That's perfectly right," said Callaghan. "Mrs. Dencourt stole it. She stole it three weeks before she left her husband. Well, what about it?"

Dencourt interrupted: "What the devil do you mean . . . what about it?"

Callaghan said: "Mr. Dencourt, if you can control yourself enough to listen I am sure Detective-Inspector Gringall will inform you that under English law a husband can't bring a charge of theft against his wife in respect of any goods which she may have taken while she was living with him. Is that right, Mr. Gringall?"

"I'm afraid that's right, Mr. Dencourt," said Gringall.

"But she's not living with me now. She's brought an action against me for divorce."

"That's true enough," said Callaghan. "And you want that divorce action to go through, don't you, Dencourt, so that you can marry this other woman you're keen on. Well, I don't think that'll be possible."

"What do you mean?" demanded Dencourt.

Callaghan smiled. He said amiably: "Well, Dencourt, I've advised Mrs. Dencourt to withdraw her divorce petition and to return to you. How do you like that?"

Dencourt was red in the face. "You can't get away with this!" he stuttered.

Gringall said quietly: "I told you Callaghan was very clever, Mr. Dencourt."

"I want that stiletto," Dencourt shouted.

Callaghan said: "I'm awfully sorry you can't have it. Mrs. Dencourt's lost it. She doesn't know where it is."

Dencourt appealed to Gringall. "Can they get away with this, Inspector?"

"I'm afraid they can, Mr. Dencourt," said Gringall. "Your wife admits that she removed that dagger at a time when she was living with you, you can't bring an action against her. If she withdraws her divorce petition and returns to you, she need not even return the stiletto. If on the other hand her divorce petition goes through then you could in the normal course of events proceed against her for the return of the stiletto. But you can't do that if she's lost it. To lose it, Mr. Dencourt, is merely carelessness, not a criminal offence."

"This is nothing but a blackmailing trap," muttered Dencourt.

Callaghan said: "Call it what you like, Dencourt. What are you going to do about it? You're a fine one to talk of blackmailing, aren't you? Look at your treatment of your wife."

Gringall interrupted. "Mr. Dencourt, I'm afraid this is a matter in which the police cannot intervene. In law, Mrs. Dencourt is still your wife, because her divorce action is not yet completed. I'm afraid the matter is one for arrangement between you and her. Perhaps she'll find the stiletto," he concluded sarcastically.

Nikolls grinned. "Find nothin'," he said. "She's lost her memory."

Gringall got up. "Sorry I can't help you, Mr. Dencourt," he said. "Good morning, Callaghan. Things are pretty good, aren't they?" He grinned at Callaghan over Dencourt's head.

Callaghan said: "Not too bad, Gringall. Thanks for coming in."

"Yeah," said Nikolls. "Come in again sometime."

As the door closed behind Gringall, Dencourt turned again to Callaghan. "Damn you, Callaghan," he said furiously. "What are you going to do?"

Callaghan said: "What can I do, Dencourt? One of these fine days with a bit of luck Mrs. Dencourt might even find that stiletto. Something might happen to refresh her memory. Then she might remember where she 'mislaid' it."

Dencourt said bitterly: "What would it take to refresh her memory?"

"Twenty thousand five hundred pounds, Dencourt," Callaghan said cheerfully. "A cheque for twenty thousand for your wife, which she richly deserves for having spent so much of her life with a blackguard like you. And five hundred pounds for Callaghan Investigations 'for services rendered.' If you don't like it," he concluded coldly, "get out!"

"If I pay this money," said Dencourt, "when shall I have the stiletto?"

Callaghan said: "I can't answer that question now, but I'm certain that when your cheque is cleared Mrs. Dencourt's memory will start working. And I have no doubt that she will continue with her divorce action."

Dencourt turned to his wife. "Do you agree to all this, Marian?"

She nodded. "Why . . . yes, Herbert," she said sweetly, "anything that Mr. Callaghan says . . ."

"Very well," said Dencourt angrily, "the cheque shall be here this afternoon. I'd like to tell you what I think of you, Callaghan." He got up.

"Don't worry, sourpuss," said Nikolls. "He's been told before, plenty!"

Callaghan said: "I shall expect your cheque this afternoon, Dencourt. Make it an open one." He called: "Effie!"

Effie Thompson appeared in the doorway. "Show Mr. Dencourt out, please."

Dencourt, with a last furious look at his wife, followed Effie from the room. As the door closed, Nikolls said with a sigh of relief: "Boy! Am I glad he's gone!"

"Why, Windy?" asked Callaghan.

Nikolls said: "The Dencourt stiletto . . ."

Callaghan grinned. He said: "What about the stiletto?"

"What about it!" said Nikolls. "I've been sittin' on the damned thing!"

12

VENGEANCE WITH A TWIST

NIKOLLS took a chubby cigar from his waistcoat pocket, bit off the end, spat it out artistically, lit the cigar and looked at Callaghan through a cloud of blue smoke. "The guy's screwy," he said. "He's just about ripe for the nut-house. I told him that you wouldn't be inclined to take a case that was already sewn up an' closed by the police, but he wouldn't listen. He says he wants vengeance, an' all he's likely to get will be a kick in the pants."

Callaghan nodded. He said: "It wouldn't be the first time we'd taken a toss with the police, Windy . . ."

"Maybe not," Nikolls answered. "But this was a suicide case all right. Dulac killed himself. Got worried or fretted about somethin' an' cut his throat. He was that sort of guy. Anyhow, the Coroner was satisfied." He inhaled a lungful of smoke with satisfaction.

Effie Thompson put her head round the office door.

"Mr. Dulac to see you," she said to Callaghan. "Mr. George Dulac . . ."

Callaghan grinned at her. "O.K., Effie. Show him in. And you can get out, Windy."

Nikolls got up. "That suits me," he said. "I got a date anyway. I'll be seein' you." He went out, whistling softly to himself.

Callaghan sat down at his desk and lit a cigarette. When Effie Thompson showed George Dulac into the office, he was busily engaged in blowing smoke rings. Effie Thompson placed a chair for the visitor and went out, closing the door quietly behind her. Callaghan watched a smoke ring as it sailed across the office. Then he tilted back his chair and looked at Dulac.

He said: "There's one thing this organization doesn't like doing, Mr. Dulac. It doesn't like bucking up against the police, and I gather from what you told my assistant yesterday that you're not very pleased with the conclusions Scotland Yard have come to. You want a case reopened."

Dulac nodded. Callaghan, who seldom felt sympathy for anyone, felt a tinge of pity for the man who sat in the big chair opposite his desk. Dulac was about fifty years of age. He looked worried and ill. His face was lined. He said: "I don't think you'll mind getting up against the police. Somehow I don't think they'll mind when they know the facts, but my lawyer says the trouble is that having come to a conclusion they won't be inclined to reopen the case. After all, that would be an admission that they were wrong."

Callaghan grinned. "If the police are wrong, they're wrong," he said. "But they aren't particularly keen on being told so by a private detective. When it's like that they take a lot of persuading." He lit a fresh cigarette. "Let me have the story from the start," he said.

Dulac gulped. Callaghan could see that his hands were trembling. There were little beads of perspiration on his forehead. After a minute he said: "As you know, Mr. Callaghan, my twin brother—Charles—committed suicide ten days ago."

Callaghan nodded. "Go on," he said.

"Charles lived by himself in a small cottage at a place called Belling—forty miles outside London." Dulac went on. "I arrived in this country two days before it happened. I was in London when I heard the news."

"Were you surprised at the idea of your brother committing suicide?" Callaghan asked.

Dulac hesitated for a moment. Then he said: "Yes and no! Let me explain what I mean. Two years ago my brother came out to South Africa to see me. He stayed at my farm in Southern Rhodesia for two or three weeks and then returned to England.

"During the time he stayed with me it was obvious that something was worrying him. Although I asked him to confide in me he would say nothing except that he had been worried by some threatening letters he had received from a man with whom he had quarreled. Immediately I heard the news of his suicide I remembered this."

"You thought that the writer of the letters might have murdered your brother?" said Callaghan. "That instead of cutting his own throat his unknown correspondent did it for him."

Dulac nodded. He went on: "The evidence at the inquest showed that people in the neighbourhood who met him on odd occasions during the two months before his death had noticed that he seemed very worried about something. Andy the coroner's jury brought in a verdict of suicide whilst of unsound mind.'

"It was only three days ago," Dulac continued, "that I went to my club. Imagine my surprise when, in the letter rack, I found a letter addressed to me in my brother's handwriting. It had apparently been written three or four weeks before. Read it for yourself."

He passed the sheet of notepaper across the desk to Callaghan, who read:

The Cottage,

Belling.

Dear George,

I am terribly worried and I hope you will arrive home in time to, be able to help me. I have had more threatening letters from a man in this neighbourhood. I believe that an attempt will be made on my life. I would be grateful if you would come down here immediately you arrive in England. Phone me on your arrival.

Yours ever,

Charles.

Callaghan re-folded the letter, put it on the desk in front of him. He said: "He talks about more threatening letters. So he'd probably received some after his visit to you in South Africa two years ago. But by now he was really frightened, was expecting something really unpleasant to happen." He stubbed out his cigarette, lit a fresh one. "Tell me, Mr. Dulac," he went on, "what sort of man was your brother?"

Dulac shrugged his shoulders. "He was very like me in appearance," he said. "I told you we were twins. But he did not scare easily. I know of nothing in his life that could come back on him. Yet there must have been something."

Callaghan said: "So it seems. And you feel certain in your mind that he was murdered?"

Dulac nodded. "I feel quite certain about that," he said. "Something tells me that Charles was killed. I want you to find his murderer, Mr. Callaghan."

Callaghan said: "I'll do my best, but it'll be like hunting for a needle in a haystack. If the police couldn't find any evidence, I don't see how we can." He blew another smoke ring. "Tell me something," he went on, "is there anybody who would benefit by your brother's death? Had he any estate to leave?"

"Not very much," said Dulac. "But everything he had is left to me."

Callaghan nodded. "That rules that angle out," he said. He thought for a while. "All right, Mr. Dulac," he said. "I'll send somebody down to Belling. We'll make a few enquiries. Who has the keys of the cottage?"

Dulac got up. He felt in his overcoat pocket, produced a bunch of keys. "I have them here," he said. "The police handed them over to me when they were through with their investigation."

"All right," said Callaghan. "I'll get in touch with you, Mr. Dulac, when we have some news." He got up.

Dulac said: "Thank you very much, Mr. Callaghan. I shall never be happy till my brother's murderer is found. I know he was murdered."

Callaghan said: "Well, if there's a murderer, we'll try and find him. In the meantime take it easy, Mr. Dulac. You're worrying too much. You need a bromide."

Dulac smiled wryly. "Possibly," he said. "This business has affected me terribly."

He put out his hand to pick up his hat from the corner of the desk, then dropped it on the floor. Callaghan retrieved it, handed it back to him. "You go home and have a rest," he said. "These days aren't particularly good for nervous people. And don't worry. We'll get in touch with you."

After Dulac had gone Callaghan went back to his chair, put his feet up on the desk and smoked silently. He seemed particularly interested in his finger-tips.

After a while he rang the bell. When Effie Thompson came in he said: "When Nikolls comes in give him these keys. Tell him to go down to Belling. Tell him it's about that suicide case that happened there ten days ago—Charles Dulac.

"And he's got to get around the neighbourhood and find out what he can about the dead man. Tell him to go over that cottage with a tooth-comb. He might find something."

She nodded and went out. Callaghan lit another cigarette and resumed his examination of his fingertips. Then he went to the telephone and asked "enquiry" for the number of the Belling Police Station.

Callaghan was drinking his afternoon cup of tea when Nikolls came in the office.

"Well, Windy," said Callaghan, "what do you know?"

"Charles Dulac went to 'The Cottage' at Belling two years ago. Nobody there knows very much about him. He never spoke to anybody. He seemed a secretive sort of cuss. Such people as did talk to him say that he seemed good an' frightened about something. I don't know what but I can make a guess."

Callaghan said: "Did you find anything in the cottage?"

"No," said Nikolls, "not a thing." He grinned. "You didn't expect me to find anything, did you?" he said. "After the police had been there. Anyhow, I reckon that Charles was scared because not so long ago he sent a cable to George. The cable was sent over the telephone from 'The Cottage' and I got a duplicate from the cable company."

"Ah!" said Callaghan. "What did it say?"

"The cable said: 'You can come back now, Charles.' It was sent to George in South Africa."

Callaghan nodded. "So George came over," he said. "He went to his club and got a delayed letter from Charles, who was by this time dead."

"That's right," said Nikolls. He went on: "I've found something else out though. Before Charles went to live at Belling—two years ago he was living in a place thirty miles away. I went over there. Charles had an enemy all right—a guy called Prosser. He had it in for Charles."

"I see," said Callaghan. "Prosser is probably the fellow who wrote the threatening letters."

"Right," said Nikolls. "Prosser admits it. He said he wrote unsigned threatening letters to Charles just to annoy him and because he knew that somebody else was after Charles, too. Prosser says Charles pinched a girl off some feller years ago, an' this feller swore he'd get back on him some time."

Callaghan said: "That's as maybe, but Prosser might be trying to alibi himself."

"He's not," said Nikolls. "Prosser didn't kill Charles. He's got a cast-iron alibi. He was in Edinburgh the week that Charles died."

Callaghan grinned. "I see," he said. "Well, that lets Prosser out."

He lit a cigarette. Nikolls got up and stretched. "Well, I hope it makes sense to you," he said. "I think this guy, George Dulac, is nutty. I think Charles was just frightened of somebody or other and decided to cut his throat."

"Yes?" said Callaghan. "That's what you think." He went over to the bookshelf, brought down a directory of insurance companies. "You take that outside, Windy," he said, handing the book to Nikolls, "and find out if any member of the Dulac family had an insurance policy."

Effie Thompson put her head round the door. She said to Callaghan: "I've got Mr. George Dulac. He's on his way round now."

"All right," said Callaghan.

He got up, walked across the corridor to Nikolls's room. He said: "Dulac'll be here in a few minutes. You'd better come in."

Nikolls grinned. He said: "So you've decided that Charles did commit suicide! I hope George won't be disappointed."

Callaghan said: "I hope he won't."

He went back into the outer office, gave some instructions to Effie Thompson. He was seated at his desk smoking when George Dulac came in. Dulac stood just inside the doorway. Callaghan thought he looked very tired.

"Well, Mr. Dulac," he said. "We've investigated the circumstances leading up to your brother's death. We've gone back a long way, too. I've found out that before he went to Belling he was living in another place thirty miles away, that he had two enemies—one, a man named Prosser, and another man Prosser suggests also disliked Charles."

Dulac said: "Then Prosser might have killed my brother?"

"Oh, no," said Callaghan. "He couldn't have. He was in Edinburgh."

Dulac said: "What about the other man?"

"He didn't do it either," Callaghan said. "Sit down, Mr. Dulac, you look tired."

"I'm not tired," said Dulac. "I'm just worried about this thing. It's obvious to me that you, like the police, believe that Charles killed himself."

Callaghan grinned. "I never said so," he said. "In fact I know that Charles did not kill himself."

"So you agree he was murdered?"

"I don't agree with that either," said Callaghan. "The man calling himself Charles Dulac, who has been living at Belling for the last two years, isn't dead. I'm talking to him now."

He stood looking down at his client. "Take it easy, George," he said. "Getting excited won't get you anywhere."

Dulac said: "I'm not getting excited. I think you're mad."

Callaghan said amiably: "No, I'm not. Let me tell you about it. Two years ago you were living in South Africa. Charles, your twin brother, was living over here. He was worried by some anonymous threatening letters that he was receiving from Prosser, and he probably wrote and told you about it.

"You got in touch with him and told him to come and see you at your farm. I imagine that when he got there he was pretty nearly a nervous wreck, and out of your brotherly love you conceived an idea to give him a rest.

"You told him that he could stay on at the farm as you—George Dulac—and that you would come over here and be Charles, that you would settle with this annoying fellow, Prosser. You came over here and you moved directly to Belling where no one would know you. You took a cottage in the name of Charles Dulac. Everybody believed you were Charles.

"You insured your life for £20,000. You waited a couple of years, and then you thought the time was ripe to strike. So you sent the real Charles in South Africa a cable saying: 'You can come back,' meaning it was safe for him to return. Then you wrote that letter to yourself and sent it to your club.

"When Charles arrived in England he went straight to Belling. That same night you killed him, came up to town and registered at an hotel as George Dulac, just arrived from South Africa. The next day you went down to Belling.

"When you got there the 'suicide' had already been discovered. Some days later you called at your club and got the letter you had written yourself which you showed to me."

Callaghan grinned. "It was too bad," he said, "that you made a mistake in the date. If you'd waited another three weeks . . ."

Dulac said hoarsely: "What the hell do you mean?"

"You were going to collect the twenty thousand pounds insurance," Callaghan went on, "on the policy you took out two years ago on your own life in the name of Charles Dulac. Unfortunately for you, you made a mistake in the date. The insurance company will pay on a suicide claim, but only two complete years after the policy is taken out. This policy had only been going one year and forty-eight weeks.

"When you realized this you were in a jam. There was only one thing to do, try and prove that Charles had been murdered. You thought you'd be safe. You imagined that the production of that letter would indicate to the police that it had been murder and not suicide, and that you'd draw the insurance money. But, of course, you had to slip up."

Dulac said: "I see. So I slipped up." He grinned sardonically. "I should like to know how," he said.

Callaghan said: "When you first came to see me, you knocked your hat off the edge of my desk. I picked it up for you. When you'd gone I found the tips of my fingers were stained with the dye from the sweat-band of your hat. I wondered why you'd decided to dye your hair.

"I got an idea. I rang through to the Belling police and asked them if there was anything odd about the body they found in the cottage. There was. It seems that for some reason best known to himself, Charles had dyed his hair black.

"Of course," Callaghan continued, "you didn't know about that until the night you killed him and then you decided that you'd better' dye your hair black, too, so that you could go back to the farm in Rhodesia as him."

He felt in his pocket for a cigarette.

"So long, Dulac," he said. "You'll find a couple of plain clothes men outside. You wanted us to persuade the police that Charles Dulac didn't commit suicide, that he was murdered. Well, we've done it, and I hope you're satisfied."

THE END